Artwork: Designs by Dana

Publisher: Paper Gold Publishing

SPARE ROOM

THE TROUBLE WITH TRIADS #1

E.M. DENNING

1

BEN

Sometimes Tristan ran on the treadmill like he could escape the demons of his job. He often brought his work as a paramedic home with him. Today, however, that wasn't the case and Ben entered the third bedroom they'd converted into a mini gym to find his husband jogging at a leisurely pace.

Ben took a moment to admire the scenery. After five years together, one of those married, Ben didn't think he'd ever tire of looking at Tristan. The treadmill stopped and Tristan took a drink from his water bottle before turning around.

"Shit!" Tristan barked and backed up a step, clutching his chest. "Warn a guy first." Tristan's surprise melted away, and he smiled at Ben.

"If I warned you, that would defeat the purpose of sneaking in here to watch you run."

Tristan smirked at Ben and stepped closer. Tristan grabbed the front of his shorts and gave his cock a squeeze. "Like to watch, do you?"

Ben made a noise in the back of his throat. "You know I do. But not now. We need to shower and get on the road or we'll miss our reservation."

"Reservation? Why, Mister Stuart, are you going to wine and dine me?" Tristan stepped into Ben's personal space and brushed the tip of his nose against Ben's.

"Get in the shower, Tristan. I hate being late."

Tristan's eyes sparkled with a combination of amusement and lust. "Can we shower together?" Tristan purred, moving closer.

Ben felt tempted, but they had a wedding anniversary to celebrate. "You have fifteen minutes to shower and dress." Ben punctuated the declaration with a kiss. "I already showered."

"But I like showering with you." Tristan pouted. His brown eyes took on a puppy-like look he'd convinced himself got him his own way more often than it actually did.

"And we'll never make it out of the shower." Ben ushered Tristan out of the room.

"You say that like it's a bad thing." Tristan sighed. "I'll be done soon, I promise."

Tristan kept his word and fourteen minutes later came down the stairs in a pair of dark slacks which accentuated his lean legs and a burgundy button up that brightened Tristan's complexion until he practically glowed.

Ben would never get over how handsome Tristan was and how lucky he was to have found him. Ben had just moved here, leaving his old life in Seattle behind him after the death of his uncle. His uncle had been the other black sheep of the family and had left Ben his house. Ben quit his job, sold most of his belongings and drove across the country, escaping his barely tolerant family.

The minute he met Tristan, the rest was history.

Ben held his hand out for his husband, who took it and brought it to his lips. Tristan kissed Ben's knuckles then stepped in closer, smelling of Christian Dior, the one Ben bought him for Christmas. Tristan liked expensive scents, but he was eternally frugal and refused to buy them, making it the perfect gift.

"You look amazing." Ben couldn't resist kissing him again. He loved all the ways Tristan kissed. Sometimes he smiled against Ben's lips. Other times he melted, turning to putty, opening for Ben beautifully. Sometimes he was ferocious and hungry, insatiable.

Today, Tristan kissed him with the hint of a smile that conveyed his uncontainable joy.

"Ready, husband?" Ben asked. The temptation to say fuck the reservations and take Tristan to bed bloomed in his chest, but hunger prevailed. Bed could wait, reservations wouldn't.

"Ready, husband." Tristan gave him another smiling kiss and grabbed his keys off the hook.

Ben retrieved their jackets and helped Tristan into his before shrugging into his own. On the way out the door, Tristan's phone buzzed in his pocket.

He gave Ben a knowing look. "Don't worry, it's not work." He fished his phone out and smiled at the screen before flashing it Ben's way. "Alex says happy anniversary."

"How's Alex?" Alex was Tristan's ex-boyfriend. They hadn't been together since they were both in their twenties. Alex had moved away and Tristan had stayed, wanting to be close to his family. By the time Alex moved back, Tristan and Ben were on their way to the altar.

Tristan shrugged, tapped out a quick reply and shoved his phone back in his pocket. "He's been weird lately. Quiet. Not himself. I've asked him if he was okay, but you know Alex," Tristan shrugged.

Ben did know Alex, but not well. "You should go for drinks with him on your next days off, see if you can cheer him up."

Tristan stopped short of the car and looked at Ben. Love poured from his soft expression. "You're a good husband."

"You're a good friend, and it sounds like Alex needs one."

"God, I haven't been out for a drink in forever. I'm already dreading the hangover."

On the way to the restaurant, Tristan tapped out a text to Alex, presumably inviting him out.

"Did you invite him?" Ben asked. He turned on his left turn signal and moved over to the turn lane. He stopped for the red light and looked at Tristan, who was still texting.

"Yeah. He's surprised I'm asking. Wants to know if it's okay with you." The corner of Tristan's lip twitched.

"I'm sure I can manage to contain my jealousy, since I suggested it in the first place."

Tristan snorted. "He's being courteous. He doesn't want to step on any toes."

By the time they arrived at the restaurant, Tristan had convinced Alex to go out with him next weekend. This put Tristan at ease and the furrow between his eyes smoothed. Had tonight been any other night, Ben might have suggested Tristan go see his friend sooner, but this was their night and Ben wanted his husband all to himself.

The restaurant was busy, but not loud. The spaced out tables, lush plants, and dim lights provided an intimate atmosphere, as promised by Ben's friend and employee, Maggie, who had recommended the place. Apparently the food was amazing.

Ben held Tristan's hand and led him inside where the hostess greeted them. "I have a reservation for two. Last name Stuart."

The hostess escorted them through the restaurant to a table off to one side. It was on the way to the restrooms and away from the noise of the kitchen. Ben pulled Tristan's chair out for him.

They ordered drinks and Ben reached across the table and took Tristan's hand. "I can't believe it's been a year."

"The best year." Tristan agreed, giving Ben's hand a gentle squeeze.

Their drinks arrived without fanfare, and Ben ordered their dinner for them. Tristan was happy to let him decide things like that, especially on nights like this. Nights when the promise of later hung thick between them. Delicious anticipation had Ben's cock throbbing in his pants, and he was thankful that he had a seat where no one could see his raging hard on.

A figure moved past them, and Tristan turned his head. "Was that?"

"Was that what?"

Tristan kept his gaze on the entrance to the hallway that led to the bathrooms. "I thought I saw Eric." Tristan's brow furrowed again.

Eric had been their boyfriend. They'd met him shortly after they'd gotten engaged, but when it became apparent that Tristan and Ben were going through with the wedding, Eric decided he wasn't comfortable being a third wheel and he broke up with them the minute they set a wedding date.

Tristan took the break up especially hard because he'd asked Ben to set a date. It wasn't logical, but he'd shouldered the responsibility for hurting everyone. It wasn't his fault, of course. If Eric was going to leave, it would have happened eventually. But Tristan was good at taking on responsibility that didn't belong to him.

"Eric." Tristan called out and Ben turned his head.

Eric looked… the same. Like the man who had walked out two years ago. Ben thought seeing Eric might have affected him differently. The break up had been harsh and abrupt. The loss wounded Ben. But where Ben expected to feel pain, only a calm numbness remained.

Eric didn't matter anymore. He was the past.

"Tristan. Ben. I…" Eric stumbled over his words. "How are you?"

"We're well, Eric. Thank you."

"How are you? We haven't heard from you since…" Tristan swallowed the last of his sentence, but he might as well have said it.

Eric, typical Eric, shrugged. "I'm okay. My boyfriend is waiting for me. Nice seeing you." Eric made a hasty retreat.

For a moment Ben watched Tristan, who watched Eric. Then Tristan turned to Ben. "I don't miss him. I thought I would, you know. Because sometimes I miss having that other person, you know. It was nice to have two men to come home to. Maybe I'm greedy." Tristan blushed, but then his expression darkened. "But that," Tristan motioned with a wave of his hand. "I don't miss. He was wrong for us."

"I didn't know you missed having a third." Tristan's statement didn't exactly surprise Ben. The idea had floated through his own mind a time or two since the wedding, but they hadn't talked about the possibility again and Ben wasn't sure how to bring it up. It didn't seem important. He was deliriously happy with Tristan.

Tristan put his hand out and waited for Ben to take it. "I didn't know either. But I saw Eric, and while I don't miss him, I miss the idea of him. Does that make sense?"

Ben nodded. "We can talk about opening up and looking for a third, if that's what you want."

Tristan shrugged. "You don't mind? Because I love you, Ben. I don't want you to think I don't or that you're not enough."

"Babe, love. Stop. I know. We've had a third before, and if it's something you want again, we can try again, okay. We have experience now, maybe next time we'll make fewer mistakes. But I don't want you to feel bad. We're grown men, we're allowed to want things, even if other people don't understand or approve."

Tristan nodded, then in typical Tristan fashion, he smiled and changed the subject. Ben might not have let it slide, but tonight was their anniversary and upsetting his husband was the last thing Ben wanted.

They ate and talked and when it came time for dessert Tristan looked at Ben with a twinkle in his eye. "Are we getting dessert here or at home?"

Ben stared Tristan down until he squirmed in his seat. "This isn't the place for the type of dessert I want."

"God, I was hoping you'd say that." Tristan exhaled and stood. "I need to use the bathroom, but I'll be right out."

"I'll get the check. Hurry back."

Tristan bent and brushed a kiss against Ben's lips.

There wasn't a thing Ben wouldn't do for that man. Tonight, he'd give him pleasure and all the love he possessed. And later, he'd see about finding someone who could fit into their life.

2

TRISTAN

Ben's breath was hot against the back of Tristan's neck. He liked how Ben towered over him a little, that he was wider and thicker and bulkier than Tristan. His thick arms wrapped around Tristan from behind and Tristan looked down, watching the muscles in Ben's arms flex and twitch as he unfastened Tristan's slacks.

Ben's arm was covered in a layer of dark hair and Tristan watched Ben's hand vanish down the front of Tristan's pants. His muscular hand took hold of Tristan's cock and he squeezed. Tristan wanted to double over, but Ben's arm wrapped around his chest and he held him still.

Ben purred, and stubble grazed against his ear. "You've been a very good husband, haven't you?"

Tristan leaned back and let Ben support him.

"I hope so." Tristan closed his eyes and fell into the sensation of Ben's hands on him. The one on his chest slid upward and wrapped around his throat. Ben squeezed gently, but enough to get Tristan's attention.

Ben squeezed Tristan's cock. Hard. And it hurt. And it shouldn't have turned Tristan on, but it did. The sharp sudden edge of pain followed by the soothing freedom when Ben released his grip.

"Shit." Tristan moaned.

Ben nipped at Tristan's ear and a shiver shot down his spine.

"You're antsy tonight." Ben stated, his voice thick with dominance. Tristan loved it when his husband got bossy in bed. It thrilled Tristan to his bones when Ben took charge.

Without warning, Ben shoved Tristan's pants down and let them pool around his ankles. He unbuttoned Tristan's shirt and pulled it down his arms. He divested Tristan of the garment and manhandled Tristan over to the bed, where he unceremoniously bent him over.

Tristan grunted when Ben pressed his chest down into the mattress with a firm hand between the shoulder blades. Tristan dug his toes into the plush carpet and sucked in a breath. He heard the clink of a belt buckle, then the sound of leather sliding through belt loops.

Tristan's cock leaked where it lay trapped against the bed. He loved not knowing what to expect. Sometimes Ben was gentle with Tristan to the point of frustration. Other times he was commanding, demanding, harsh, and strict. And Tristan loved it all. Tonight, Ben was intense and Tristan's balls drew up tight to his body in anticipation of the release Tristan might not get because Ben didn't always let him come. Coming was great, but sometimes, not coming was better. More than delicious. Salacious. To be strung out and pulled tight and left straining and wanting.

Fingers probing his hole brought Tristan's attention back to his body. Blunt and dry, Tristan arched his back and pushed himself against them, offering his body, his hole. Whatever Ben wanted, he could have.

Tristan's eagerness earned him a sharp slap to the ass. The white-hot sting struck like lightning, but Ben did nothing to soothe it. He let Tristan bask in the flare of pain before he spread Tristan's cheeks and spit on Tristan's hole.

The blunt fingers returned, and without finesse, Ben pressed one digit inside Tristan.

"You're a tight little hole."

"Fuck, Ben. That's so hot." Tristan shamelessly humped the bed, relishing the friction.

"I'd better stretch you, or it might hurt."

Tristan buried his face in the bed and bit back a moan.

"What was that?" Ben gripped the back of Tristan's hair and yanked his head back. "Did you say something?"

"Fuck me."

A second finger joined the first, and Tristan hissed. The intrusion burned, but Ben knew how to make it hurt in a good way.

"Does that feel good?" Ben spit on Tristan's hole again and twisted his fingers.

"Fuck, yes."

The intrusion vanished and another sharp sting of pain erupted on Tristan's other ass cheek. Tristan opened his eyes and looked over his shoulder the best he could. He wanted to see Ben fuck him and own him.

Ben shoved his fingers back in Tristan's ass. The corner of his lip twitched, and then Tristan jolted as Ben stroked his fingers against Tristan's prostate.

"Fuck." Tristan bucked against the bed. His hips wouldn't stop thrusting with every stroke of Ben's fingers.

"Does my little slut need something?" Ben leaned down and purred the words against Tristan's bare shoulder. Teeth scraped across Tristan's flesh.

"You. Need you."

Ben's laugh was cruel and lusty. "My little slut always needs me."

Tristan rutted against the bed. It was almost involuntary now. He wanted to fuck, to be fucked. To have Ben bury himself deep and hard. To leave bruises the shape of his fingers on Tristan's hips and marks from his mouth on his shoulders, his chest, wherever Ben wanted to leave them. He loved all the different kinds of sex they had, but Tristan absolutely adored being Ben's slut.

"What does my little slut need?"

"Your cock. Please. I need it in me." Tristan tried to spread his legs wider but was hindered by his pants, still in a pool around his ankles. "Please fuck me." Tristan closed his eyes and begged.

Ben lined his cock up and slowly eased his way in to Tristan. Lubed only with spit, Tristan dug his toes into the plush carpet and clenched his teeth, losing himself in the slow, agonizing stretch.

By the time Ben's cock got fully seated inside Tristan, a thin sheen of sweat had layered his skin. He panted, open-mouthed into the bed. Ben pressed his hands into Tristan's shoulders and shoved him deeper into the bed, then thrust.

Tristan could do nothing but stay there and take it.

Ben called him names. Delicious, dirty ones like slut and whore. He spoke words that shouldn't mean as much as they did, but they were everything to Tristan. He loved having Ben wild and unruly above him, in him. Owning him and using him. He liked how Ben felt safe enough and secure enough with him to call him names, to get in his ear and whisper obscenities.

Tristan shook with the need to release, but he held back. Waiting for those sweet words Ben would say to him. Ben came, hard and long and unrelenting. He fucked Tristan until his feet no longer touched the floor and he had to put one knee on the bed to follow Tristan's body.

"Please, please can I come?"

"No." Ben said. He pulled his cock free of Tristan's ass. "Don't move."

He wasn't gone long and when he returned, the blunt end of a plug pressed at Tristan's entrance. He slid it in and then pressed on it, making Tristan groan.

Tristan drifted to the other side of his agony while Ben untangled his pants from his ankles. He tossed the clothing in the basket in the corner, then finished stripping out of his own clothing.

Tristan rolled over and reached for his dick, but a sharp look from Ben stilled his hand.

"Did I say you could touch my things?"

"You're mean." Tristan pouted

Ben reached for Tristan and grabbed his hand. He tugged it to his lips and kissed the golden wedding band that glimmered on his finger. "You're not to come until tomorrow morning when I fuck my load out of your ass."

Tristan sighed and tossed his free arm over his eyes. "You're too good to me."

"Come on, I'll wash your back." Ben tugged Tristan to his feet. Were it not for Ben, Tristan would roll over and go to sleep, covered in sweat and still throbbing with need. But Ben made sure Tristan washed the sweat away. He rubbed body wash into Tristan's skin, massaged his shoulders, and even bent and carefully washed between Tristan's toes.

The dichotomy of Ben never failed to make Tristan's dick hard. Most often, they had sweet sex. Long strokes and whispered endearments. Laughter. But sometimes Ben liked to shove Tristan face first into the mattress and choke him with his cock, or pin him down and fuck him senseless one minute, and in the next, he could worship Tristan. Bathe him. Attend to needs so small, Tristan wasn't aware he had them. He supposed both sides of the coin were a type of worship, but Tristan never stopped being fascinated by his husband.

"I love you." Tristan said to Ben as he wrapped a fluffy towel around Tristan and rubbed his skin dry.

"I love you, too." Ben stole a kiss, then went back to drying Tristan off.

How could Tristan possibly want more than this? Ben was

perfect. He was doting and caring and sweet. His heart was bigger than anyone's. He was everything Tristan wanted. Standing naked, being pampered and doted on by his husband, had guilt gnawing at Tristan's stomach.

"I'm sorry." Tristan blurted, unable to contain himself.

Ben stopped drying him off and raised his head to look him in the eyes.

"For what?" Ben cupped Tristan's cheek, and Tristan leaned into the touch.

"For thinking we need someone else. We don't. We're fine." Tristan was on the verge of babbling and he made himself be quiet.

Ben regarded him thoughtfully. "You have nothing to be sorry for."

"But..."

"No buts. We're fine. We were fine before Eric, we were fine with Eric, and we're fine without him. If we decide we want to open our marriage and look around for a partner, it will be a decision we'll make together. Okay?"

"I don't want you to think you're not enough." Tristan confessed. He hated being honest sometimes. The vulnerability sliced him open. But if he couldn't be honest with his husband, who could he be honest with?

"I would never think that." Ben drew Tristan close and wrapped his arms around him. "You'd never think that about yourself, would you?"

"No." Tristan sighed and leaned into Ben's embrace. "I know you love me. It's in everything you say and do."

"Then trust that works both ways, love. Okay?"

"Okay." Tristan closed his eyes and absorbed the kiss that Ben pressed to the side of his head.

"Come on. Let's get to bed."

"But I'm not sleepy." Tristan protested.

"Who says I was going to let you sleep?" Ben pulled away and tugged the towel off Tristan. He motioned to the bedroom. "Get into bed. I'll be right there."

Tristan climbed under the covers and scooted to the middle of the king sized bed. A bed that felt too big and too empty until Ben climbed in beside him a minute later. Tristan rolled over and curled into Ben's side. He slung an arm around Ben's waist and despite the protest that he wasn't sleepy, Tristan fell asleep in moments.

3

ALEX

Alex scrubbed the fatigue from his face and took a breath of fresh air when he stepped off the bus and onto the street in front of the bar where he was meeting Tristan at. Drinks were a bad idea. Scratch that. Drinks with Tristan were a bad idea.

Tristan was married. And happy. And of course, his husband was this perfect, non-jealous, non-controlling man who didn't care if Tristan went for drinks with an ex. Alex wanted to hate him, but Tristan deserved someone like that.

Alex paid the cover charge, stepped into the bar, then made a beeline for one of the empty stools and sat down. He'd scanned the place on his way in and hadn't spotted Tristan. He ordered a draft from the bartender and paid cash. There was no way he could afford to open a tab tonight. Maybe if his clients paid him on time, he could afford to take an Uber to the bar and open a tab. But a bus and two beers were all he could spare.

Alex scrubbed a hand down his face and exhaled. He shouldn't be here. He should leave. Tristan would understand. Alex didn't fit into his life anymore. It was shameful the way Alex stalked Tristan online. Through his online profiles, Alex had watched him and his husband fall in love and get married. He watched Tristan get everything he ever wanted. Everything he deserved. Why he still wanted to be friends with Alex, he didn't know.

Alex moved to stand when someone touched his shoulder.

"Alex. Hi, oh my god, how are you?" Tristan's smiling face greeted him a second before Tristan pulled Alex into an embrace. He stood there, stunned and awkward for a moment before he snapped out of his stupor and returned the hug.

When they separated, Tristan took the stool next to him and ordered a beer and a shot. "How are you? I know we've barely talked lately. Work has been insane." Tristan grimaced at the mention of his job and downed the shot the minute the bartender set it in front of him.

Alex tried not to look at Tristan too much, because that's all he wanted to do. He felt like a fucking creep. Tristan was his ex. His married ex and Alex was a loser who carried a torch and nursed an old flame. But Tristan was beautiful. His light brown hair always looked soft and fluffy. A couple of grays colored a patch near his temple, and his once youth-smooth face had crow's feet and laugh lines. He looked good for thirty-five, but he still looked thirty-five and not the twenty something Alex had left behind.

"I'm okay. You look good." Alex blushed and looked down at his half empty drink. He didn't even remember drinking the first half. "I mean, you look happy. How was your anniversary?"

"It was good. Ben took me for dinner. That's the part of the evening I can share." Tristan winked at him. "The rest can't be discussed in public, it's impolite, but I think I've finally recovered from it."

Jealousy burned through Alex. There was a time when Tristan had been his and Alex had been a fucking fool. He'd traded his heart for a taste of success, and in the end, got left with nothing. The recession had hit Alex hard. He ended up losing his job, his house, his life. He left with everything and came back with nothing.

"I'm happy for you." The words hurt to say, but they were honest. Alex might hate the idea that Tristan found happiness with someone else, but Tristan deserved it. All the parts of Alex that never stopped loving Tristan wanted him to be happy.

"Are you okay?"

The question shouldn't have shocked Alex. Tristan knew him. Even after all these years, picking their friendship up had been easy. He'd sent Tristan a message one night shortly after he moved back to town, and though Alex refused to let Tristan know exactly where he lived, they'd kept in touch.

"I'm alright." Alex forced a smile.

"Wow. That's the saddest lie you've ever told me." Tristan ordered a pitcher of beer and when it arrived, he tapped Alex's arm. "Let's grab a table."

Alex didn't argue. There wasn't a point when dealing with Tristan. He had a knack for getting his own way.

Alex sat down in the booth across from Tristan and against his better judgement, drained his second drink. Draft beer was crap, but Alex hadn't drunk in years and he was already feeling off kilter by the end of his second drink. Warm and fuzzy around the edges, if not slightly more maudlin than when he'd come in. God, he hoped he didn't cry or worse, confess his love to Tristan.

"What's going on with you?" Tristan asked.

"What makes you think something's going on?" Alex filled his glass and tried to wipe the image of a twenty-two-year-old Tristan from his mind. The Tristan that had belonged to him. That he'd thrown away. Hindsight was twenty-twenty, and seeing what he'd thrown away sucked. Tristan had been his, but he'd wanted things and money. He'd put his ego ahead of his relationship and he'd never been sorrier.

"You've been quiet lately. Withdrawn. Not yourself. I'm worried about you."

Alex shrugged. "I'm fine."

"And still a lousy liar. Come on, Alex, you can tell me."

Alex shook his head. "We should play." Alex motioned to the pool tables next to them. Two sat empty. Alex sucked at pool, but anything was better than sitting around trying not to stare at Tristan. He felt like Tristan could see right through him sometimes, and if he looked too long, too hard, all of Alex's secrets would come tumbling out into the light of day.

And it would ruin their delicate friendship. Tristan was the one good thing Alex had left, and having him as a friend was far better than not having him at all.

Alex half expected Tristan to argue with him. Instead, Tristan flashed him a wide, dazzling smile. "You're on." Tristan said as he got to his feet. "I hope you've gotten better over the years or I'm still going to kick your ass."

"I can promise you I haven't." Alex laughed and retrieved a couple of cues from the rack on the wall and passed one to Tristan.

"Oh god. This is going to be a bloodbath, isn't it?"

Alex shrugged. "Some things never change."

The night went slightly better for Alex once they started playing pool. It felt almost like old times. Tristan's laughter rang bright in Alex's ears when Alex made the cue ball jump off the table. All of Alex's shots went wide, or came up short, or bounced around and hit nothing at all.

Tristan beat him in every game and the more Alex drank, the worse he got. When the pitcher was empty Tristan offered to buy him another drink, but Alex shook his head. His face hurt from smiling and as much as he didn't want this night to end, Alex was too drunk to continue on without embarrassing himself.

He'd forgotten how easy it was to be around Tristan. Their friendship felt effortless, like no time had passed and they were still the same men they were years ago. Laughing and drinking and falling into bed together.

Alex needed to get out of there before he said or did something stupid. Tristan was taken. Married. Happy. Maybe one day, Alex could be, too.

"I should get going." Alex said as he put his cue back into the rack he got it from.

"Are you sure?"

"It's almost midnight and I've had more to drink today than I have in a while."

"At least have a drink with me while you wait for an Uber." Tristan batted those ridiculous eyelashes of his and Alex nodded before he thought better of it.

Tristan ordered Alex a shot of something, he didn't pay attention to what. Alex didn't have the money for an Uber, not really, but there was no way he could make it home on the bus. Not when the world already tilted beneath his feet. And then the alcohol from the shot hit Alex's bloodstream. It warmed him through and a few minutes later he was grateful for the chilly night air when they stepped outside to meet his Uber.

"I had fun." Tristan slung an arm around Alex and pulled him into an embrace. This time it was awkward for different reasons. Alex had been half hard all night. Watching Tristan bend and stretch to play pool had Alex's cock twitching in his pants. The torture had been exquisite but wholly inappropriate. Just like it would be to jerk off to the memory of this innocent hug. He hoped Tristan's cologne clung to him forever.

Okay, Alex was far too drunk for his own good. Lucky for him, the Uber he ordered pulled up and gave him an excuse to pull out of their hug.

"It was good to see you." Alex said in lieu of all the things he wanted to say, but couldn't. Shouldn't. Shouldn't even think.

Tristan squeezed Alex's shoulder. "It was good to see you, too. Don't be a stranger, okay?"

Alex nodded. "Okay. I won't." Alex promised, but he wasn't sure if it was a lie or not. Seeing Tristan had been great, glorious even. And maybe for those reasons, Alex shouldn't hang out with him anymore.

He climbed into the Uber with a smile on his face and let it stay there until the Uber pulled away and Alex gave him his address. Then he leaned back and closed his eyes and tried to keep the world from spinning him off the surface.

The climb to his third-floor apartment nearly killed him, but the elevator had been out for six months, with no signs of the landlords getting it fixed. Alex rarely minded. It was hell for his elderly neighbor, and Alex often stopped to help him carry his groceries up the stairs, but when Alex was drunk and unsteady, it was a special sort of hell.

After he made it to his door in one piece and slid inside, he threw the deadbolt and the chain and instead of showering off his drunken state, Alex climbed into bed. He didn't bother to take his clothes off. He wouldn't. Not until he was sober and could maybe, possibly, resist the urge of grabbing his dick and jerking himself to completion with Tristan's name on his lips.

Alex curled up on top of the covers and passed out cold with his spare pillow hugged to his chest.

When Alex woke, it was still dark outside, but the world was too bright, too loud for the middle of the night. Something was wrong. He coughed and blinked the sting from his eyes, then coughed again.

Too loud. Alex thought. Then it dawned on him. The fire alarm screamed, lights flashed through smoke.

Fuck. Alex rolled off his bed and threw up on his bedroom floor, suddenly aware of the strange warmth and the smell. The smoke. The sound. His building was on fire.

4

BEN

Ben woke to Tristan crawling into bed next to him. He wrapped his arms around Ben from behind and pressed his nose into the back of Ben's neck.

"Have fun?" Ben tangled his fingers with Tristan's and brought them to his lips. He brushed a kiss across the knuckles, then tucked himself tighter against Tristan.

"Mmhm. Sleepy now. Love you." Tristan kissed the back of Ben's neck and gave him a squeeze. It wasn't long before Tristan's breathing evened out and he fell asleep. Ben soon followed. His alarm would go off soon enough and he'd have to pry himself away from his warm bed, and his lovely husband and open the bookstore.

Something buzzed. Incessantly. Ben pried an eye open and wondered at the time. The sky was pre-sunrise gray and Ben didn't have to be up for another couple of hours.

Ben sat up and reached for the phone that vibrated on the nightstand where Tristan left it. Ben didn't make a habit of answering his husband's phone, but the call was coming from the hospital.

"Tristan's phone," Ben croaked quietly.

"Um... is Tristan there?" The voice on the other end sounded hoarse and rough. Who ever was on the other end was clearly upset, but it didn't sound like anyone in Tristan's family.

"Yeah, one second." Ben rolled over and placed a hand on Tristan's shoulder. "Babe, wake up."

Tristan grunted and squeezed his eyes closed. He made a sound in protest.

"The phone's for you. The call came from the hospital."

Tristan's eyes popped open and his hand flailed out of the covers until he found the phone in Ben's hand.

"This is Tristan." Tristan struggled to sit up. The covers pooled around his waist and Tristan absently scratched at his chest. Tristan went still. "Alex? What happened?" Tristan listened for a moment before he shot out of bed. "Yeah, no, it's fine. Oh my god, are you okay? You're sure? You're not hurt? What the fuck happened?"

Ben climbed out of bed and slid into a pair of jeans and a Henley. He passed Tristan a pair of pants and watched him shimmy into them, keeping the phone pinned to his ear.

"We'll be right there, okay. Where are you? Never mind, I'll find you. It's okay. Stop apologizing. Okay, see you soon." Tristan hung up the phone and looked at Ben. His eyes were wide and his face was pale. With his disheveled hair, he looked like a spooked owl. "Alex's building burned down."

"Fuck. Is he okay?"

"He's... he's okay. He says he is. They took him to the hospital as a precaution, but he's not hurt." Tristan took a deep breath. "I just saw him. I watched him get in an Uber."

Ben went to Tristan and pulled him into a hug. Tristan clung to him for a minute before he took a deep breath. "He's okay." Ben assured him. "We'll go see him and see what he needs, okay?"

Tristan nodded and mumbled a thank you against Ben's shoulder.

The emergency department at the hospital was absolute insanity and were it not for Tristan knowing every nurse in there, they might have been waiting for hours to get in to see Alex.

Alex lay in a hospital bed hooked to machines to monitor his vitals. Tristan went straight to Alex and wrapped his arms around him.

"What happened?"

"I went home and went to sleep." Alex gripped Tristan's hand. "I woke up and the whole place was burning down. There's not much to tell."

Ben highly doubted that was the case, but he looked shaken up and it wasn't Ben's place to push. What Alex needed was a shower, maybe a meal, and a good long sleep.

Tristan pulled away and glanced at the machines that beeped softly. "Your oxygen saturation is good. Your other vitals look fine." Tristan exhaled a sigh of relief.

"I told you I wasn't hurt. They wanted to check me out because I was in the building for so long."

"I'm glad you're okay." Tristan pulled the chair up to the side of Alex's bed and sat down.

"When are they releasing you?"

"As soon as the doctor comes back for another look at me. If he says I can go… but um. The building. It's gone." Alex wrapped his arms around himself and shivered. Tristan stood and pulled Alex's blanket up to his chin.

"I'm going to step out and see if I can track down your doctor, okay. I'll be right back." Tristan motioned at Ben and he followed his husband out of the cubicle and around a corner where Alex was unlikely to hear them.

"Can he stay?" Tristan asked.

"Of course." Tristan's relief was palpable, and he nearly collapsed into Ben's arms.

"I love you. You're a good man, Ben Stuart."

"How could I possibly say no, Tris?" Ben brushed a kiss against Tristan's temple. "I'm not cruel."

"Most husband's wouldn't want their husband's ex crashing in the spare room."

Ben made a sound in the back of his throat. "We both know I'm not most husbands. I'm not about to let someone be homeless. My ego can handle it."

They shared a quiet laugh, and Tristan laced his fingers with Ben's and gave his hand a squeeze. It was something Tristan often did when he had too many thoughts and couldn't articulate what he was feeling.

"We should get back in there." Ben suggested. Tristan took a deep breath and nodded.

When they returned to the cubicle, Alex still looked pale and shaken. Of course Ben would let him stay, he wasn't a monster. The man had been through hell, and he looked the part.

A doctor appeared and glanced at Tristan. "Hey, Tristan. Friend of yours?"

"Yeah."

"Well good news, your friend is fine and is free to go."

Alex immediately pulled the oxygen mask off his face and the blood pressure monitor off his finger. Tristan folded his arms over his chest and talked to the doctor, asking questions about Alex's treatment.

Ben drifted to Alex, who slung his legs over the edge of the bed and stared down at his feet.

Alex lifted his gaze to meet Ben's, and he opened his mouth. "I don't have shoes."

"We'll get you some later." Ben promised. "When they release you, I'll leave you with Tristan and I'll pull the car around."

Alex nodded and patted his clothing. "I think I have my wallet. I can get a hotel or something."

"You'll stay with us." Ben didn't give Alex the courtesy of

asking if he wanted to. Neither Ben nor Tristan would let Alex go to a hotel after what he'd been through.

Alex looked up at him with a thousand questions in his eyes.

"I promise it's fine." Ben put a hand on Alex's shoulder and gave it a squeeze.

"I... thank you." Alex said and cleared his throat.

"You're free to go." Tristan said, slipping in next to Ben. He tucked a hand in the crook of Ben's elbow, seeking the comfort of contact.

Ben turned to Tristan. "I'll bring the car around. See you in a minute."

Tristan nodded and Ben felt his gaze as he slipped out of the curtain. Tristan's soft voice said something likely reassuring to Alex, and Ben smiled at how big his husband's heart was. Sometimes he wished Tristan could compartmentalize things better, it would make his job easier on him, but that was purely selfish of Ben, who hated seeing Tristan upset about anything.

Ben pulled the car around and Tristan slid into the back seat with Alex.

"Thank you for this. I'll... figure it out. I'll be gone as soon as I can." Alex said and Tristan hushed him.

"Alex, stop. You'll stay as long as you need to, okay."

"He's right." Ben chimed in from the front seat. He pulled the car out of the hospital parking lot and into the light traffic of the early morning. "I don't know about you two, but I'm starving. I'll grab something from the drive thru on the way home."

Alex might have protested but Tristan chimed in with an enthusiasm for breakfast sandwiches, one of his greatest weaknesses. Tristan tried to stay in shape and eat healthy, but he often stated he couldn't resist the siren song of a bacon and egg sandwich.

Tristan ate his in three large bites while Alex only managed half before he tucked it back in the wrapper.

Tristan met Ben's gaze in the rearview, worry etched into his eyes. Ben was sure Alex would be fine after a shower and a proper sleep.

When they got home, Ben unlocked the door and Tristan ushered Alex inside.

"Here, let me show you where you can clean up. You'll probably fit Ben's stuff better than you'll fit mine, but we have things you can change into."

Alex blinked at Tristan, then nodded. "Yeah. Um. My stuff. I don't know when I can get it. If… there's anything…"

"Don't worry about that right now." Tristan gave Ben a pained look, then led Alex down the hallway. He chattered on, trying to reassure Alex that everything would be okay.

Ben got to work tidying the spare room. They didn't have guests often, but they kept the bed made. Sometimes Ben used the desk in the corner as an office. He opened the drawer and cleared the miscellaneous items off the surface and into the drawer. The laptop got unplugged and moved to the living room.

He met Tristan in the kitchen. The sound of the shower running got Ben's attention for a moment. He hoped it might make Alex feel better. If he felt better, Tristan might.

Ben went to him and gathered him in his arms. Tristan's hands fisted the sides of Ben's shirt.

"He could've been hurt."

"He wasn't. Let's focus on that, okay?"

Tristan nodded against Ben's shoulder. "You're going to be late if you don't leave soon."

"I'm not going in today. I hadn't even thought of it. I'll call Maggie and get her to start early. We'll open a little later, that's all." Ben kept one arm wrapped around Tristan and fumbled his phone out of his back pocket. With one hand he unlocked his phone, then called Maggie and arranged for her to open. The bookstore was only open until six most nights, and Maggie would welcome the extra hours on her check.

The shower stopped and a few minutes later Alex came

padding out in bare feet. Alex fit Ben's clothes well enough that they could have been his own. In his arms, he held his bundle of clothing. "Could we wash these?"

Ben had half a mind to suggest throwing them out, but they might be the only possessions Alex had left, so he nodded and took them from him carefully. "I'll get them washing while Tristan shows you the guest room."

"Thank you." Alex wouldn't meet Ben's gaze.

It was going to kill Ben, the way Alex kept thanking him for doing the bare minimum. He didn't want to comment on it, though. Alex had been through too much and Ben didn't want to add to his stress.

"Don't mention it. Tristan and I are happy to help."

Tristan smiled at Ben, then wrapped an arm around Alex's shoulders and steered him down the hallway. He glanced over his shoulder at Ben once Alex had disappeared into the guest room and he blew Ben a kiss.

Ben smiled back, then turned and started the load of laundry he promised. He googled the news and his breath caught in his throat when he saw images of the raging inferno Alex had walked out of. By the looks of the images in the article and the news clip he watched, the entire building was gone. Alex no longer had belongings to retrieve. Ben sighed, unsure of how he was going to tell Alex the bad news.

5

TRISTAN

Tristan doubted he'd be able to go back to sleep, but Ben climbed into bed next to him. Tristan laid his head on Ben's shoulder and soon enough Tristan drifted off to the feeling of Ben's delicate touch raking through his hair.

Tristan woke later, and he was still in bed with Ben, who sat up reading something on his phone. Once Ben sensed his husband was awake, he turned his head and pulled his reading glasses off. He set them on the nightstand. "Hey. Feel better?"

"I feel more human. What a morning." Tristan shoved himself into a sitting position, yawned, and leaned his head against Ben's shoulder. "I hope Alex got some sleep."

"I wouldn't be surprised if he didn't. He looked pretty shaken." Ben tilted his phone until the screen was in Tristan's line of sight. "The building is a total loss. The roof collapsed about an hour ago. Luckily, though several people went to the hospital, only three people suffered minor injuries and no one was killed."

Tristan looked at the destruction on the phone screen. The flames and smoke. The chaos of fire was something Tristan had witnessed as a paramedic, but he'd had the good fortune to never have lost something in a fire.

Alex, on the other hand, had lost everything.

"Fuck."

"He can stay as long as he needs to." Ben turned the phone off and set it aside, then wrapped his arms around Tristan. Tristan tried to soak in as much comfort as he could, but part of his mind screamed that he shouldn't. Guilt gnawed at him until it ate away his insides and left him hollow. Alex might have died in that fire. He almost hadn't woken up.

When Tristan was slow to respond, Ben cupped his chin and tilted his head until they made eye contact.

"What do you need?"

Tristan tried to smile, but failed. He sniffled, partly because the sight of Alex's building shook him, but also because the part of town Alex had been living in wasn't the best and the building had been awful before the fire. Tristan had been there on several calls in the past for overdoses and out-of-control violence. How had Tristan not known where his friend had been living? He wondered what else Alex was keeping from him.

He didn't have a right to know; he knew that logically, but they'd been close once. Once. Not anymore. Not since Alex left for the west coast. Tristan could've gone, in theory. But in reality, he couldn't imagine living anywhere else. He'd grown up here. He knew the businesses, the people, and his way around. He enjoyed contributing to a place that had treated him so well. And his family was here. There had been many reasons Tristan wouldn't leave, and though he kept things he'd been unwilling to give up, he'd sacrificed his relationship with Alex.

"I'm glad he called me." Tristan shoved the guilt down and almost choked on it. He'd make it all up to Alex. He'd help him get back on his feet. "I want to help him."

"Of course you do. You're a good friend."

Tristan frowned and turned to his husband. "Why do I sense a but, coming?"

"But you can't fix everything for him, Tris."

Tristan sighed and tried not to be annoyed. "I don't want to fix things for him, I want to help."

Ben draped his arm around Tristan's shoulders and pulled him closer. "I know you do, but it's like with your job, you put so much of yourself into things, and when they don't go how you want them to, it hurts you. And I don't like seeing you hurt."

"How do you know Alex is going to hurt me?" Tristan tried to be offended, but the emotion wouldn't stick. He could never get truly annoyed at Ben's concern when it came about so honestly. Tristan had suffered more than a few horrible days because of things that happened on the job, and Ben was always there to piece him back together. Ben was his rock.

"I don't know that he will, but you don't know that he won't."

"But he can still stay, right?" Tristan wriggled around and looked Ben in the eyes. He met a soft, liquid chocolate gaze.

"Of course he can."

"He's my ex." Tristan stated.

Ben appeared to be amused by this and smirked. "I'm well aware. I'm also with a man who I trust completely. I'm not worried about Alex being here."

"You're not jealous?"

Ben shook his head. "Not even a little."

Tristan leaned in and brushed the tip of his nose against Ben's scratchy stubble. "Good. I don't want this to be a problem."

"It's not. I promise."

"And if it becomes one?" Tristan put his hand over Ben's heart. "You'll tell me?"

"Honesty first and forever." Ben dragged Tristan into a toe curling kiss. He wrapped his muscular hand around the back of Tristan's neck and devoured his mouth, putting an end to the conversation and telling Tristan without words how serious he was.

Tristan and Ben showered together, which was one of Tristan's favorite things. He loved being naked and intimate with Ben in all the ways, but there was something about getting clean together Tristan could never get enough of. He'd tried to understand why a few times, but the best he could ever come up with was that he enjoyed being near Ben and having reasons to touch him. Ben also doted on Tristan when they were in the shower together, and Tristan enjoyed those moments with a childish greed.

Tristan curled up on the couch and used his phone to order a few changes of clothing for Alex and things like socks and underwear. He didn't want to go overboard and step on Alex's toes, but there were things Alex couldn't do without. Like shoes. He maybe should've discussed the purchases with Alex first, but Tristan only ordered a few things to start with. A few changes of clothing. A few sets of sleepwear and other random essentials to get him through.

It wasn't until nearly dinner time when Alex finally slipped out of the guest room. Shadows clung to his face, haunting his expression. Tristan doubted that he'd slept much. If at all.

"Hey. There's coffee." Tristan offered and Alex nodded mutely. He slipped into a chair at the kitchen table and Tristan poured him a cup. He brought it to him the way he always took it, black; no sugar. "I ordered you some clothes and stuff. They'll be here tomorrow."

Alex looked at him with round, stunned eyes and Tristan caught the expression on Ben's face when he turned to refresh his own cup of coffee. He knew he should tread carefully, as he'd planned to, but the minute Alex woke up, Tristan's urge to fix things kicked in. He couldn't stand the thought of leaving Alex sitting there in borrowed clothing, wondering when he'd have his own things again.

"Thanks." Alex choked out. His voice sounded raw and hoarse, probably from the fire. Tristan thrust that thought out of his mind and forced his hands to steady themselves as he brought the cup of coffee to his lips and took a sip.

Tristan searched his mind for something to say but kept coming up empty. He wanted to ask Alex more about the fire. He wanted to delve into the details and make sure Alex was unscathed. His body was fine, but any idiot could tell Alex had been through hell. Tristan wanted to soothe him, but didn't know how. Not anymore.

"I'll pay you back." Alex said quietly.

Tristan and Ben shared a look, and Tristan went to the table. He pulled a chair closer to Alex and set his coffee down. He kept his fingers wrapped around the mug, but they twitched with the need to put his hand in Alex's and offer him some comfort.

"You don't need to, Alex. Ben and I, we want to help."

Alex looked up and raked a hand over his face. "I don't know how I'm going to come back from this, Tristan. I can't even email my clients. Fuck."

"We have a laptop you can use, Alex. You have everything saved to the cloud, right?" Alex gave him a weak nod. "Then it's settled. You can use the laptop and stay in the spare room until we get you sorted and back on your feet."

Alex released a shaky breath. "It's too much."

"It's okay. I promise we're not offering more than we're willing to give."

Ben stood in the background, draining pasta and putting the finishing touches on dinner. The background noise offered a distraction for Alex, who looked overwhelmed. He turned in the chair to look at Ben over his shoulder.

"Whatever you're cooking, it smells amazing."

"Chicken Alfredo. There's garlic toast in the oven. I figured today was one for comfort food."

"I haven't had Alfredo in ages."

Ben smiled and dug plates out of the cupboard. "Don't get too impressed. The sauce is from a bottle. All I did was cook chicken and noodles and stir it all together."

"But you're so good at it." Tristan got up from the table and helped Ben by getting the garlic toast out of the oven and putting it on a plate. Ben set a large serving bowl down in the center of the table, then passed around the plates and forks.

He served Alex first, then Tristan, then himself. For a few minutes, dinner provided a nice distraction from the events of the day. Then Alex raised his head from his half eaten plate of food.

"The building is gone, isn't it?" Though he directed the question at Tristan, it was Ben who answered.

"I'm sorry. The roof collapsed earlier. There's no way you're going to get in there to collect any of your belongings, even if there was anything left to get."

Alex pushed the food around his plate, no longer interested in eating.

Tristan didn't know what to say to his friend. Everything that ran through his mind sounded stupid and overly positive, but in a toxic way. How could he sit there and tell someone who lost everything that it would be okay? He couldn't. He wanted to; it was the thing people said when bad things happened.

"Hey, um. Tristan. Is there a way you could find out what happened to my neighbor?" Alex asked suddenly.

"Yeah, sure, probably. What's his name?"

"George Tucker. He lived in the unit next to me. I helped him down the stairs, and he wasn't doing too good. He has COPD and I think the smoke was really hard on him. They took him in an ambulance before they took me."

Tristan nodded. "I have a shift tomorrow and I'll see what I can find out for you, okay. But if it helps, the news reported no fatalities."

The strain in Alex's shoulders eased, but didn't disappear. "It does, thanks. Do you have any aspirin? My head is killing me."

"I'll get it." Ben offered and returned a moment later with the bottle. He set it on the table and let Alex shake out a couple of pills for himself. He took them with a swallow of coffee and dinner finished in an extended, awkward silence.

Tristan and Ben shared looks across the table until Alex quietly excused himself for the night and went to bed. Tristan and Ben wished him a goodnight, then cleaned the kitchen together before curling up in front of the television in front of a show neither of them paid much attention to. And when Tristan did climb between the sheets with his husband, Ben climbed into bed and wrapped Tristan in his arms.

"He'll be okay." Ben made Tristan believe him with a kiss to the back of his neck. But it still didn't help Tristan fall asleep any easier. Not when his mind churned like a storming sea. But in the end, exhaustion won out and Tristan drifted off, clinging to Ben's quiet proclamation.

6

ALEX

Alex woke the next morning and forced himself to leave the unfamiliar room. He didn't see Tristan, but Ben was in the kitchen nursing a cup of coffee and scrolling through his phone. When Alex entered the room, Ben looked up from his phone, then set it aside.

"You missed Tristan, but there's coffee if you want some. I have to head into the bookstore for a few hours this morning, but I'll be free later if you needed to go anywhere."

Alex blinked, dug the heel of his hand into his eye and gave it a vigorous rub. "I'll be okay."

"I left my cell phone number on the fridge, Tristan's too."

"I don't have a phone." Alex mumbled and plucked a cup from the cupboard.

"We have a landline for emergencies. The portable handset is in the living room."

Alex turned and raised an eyebrow. "You have a landline?"

Ben nodded like it was the most normal thing in the world.

"No one has landlines anymore. Everyone has cellphones. Hell, you and Tristan have cell phones."

"And we have a landline for emergencies." Ben shrugged. "It

makes me feel better to have it, and it doesn't cost much. It's bundled with the internet and television service. The extra charge is negligible."

Alex cleared his throat, remembering all the work he had ahead of him sorting out his clients and his files. Seeing what he could do with the programs on the borrowed laptop would at least keep him distracted for a good part of the day.

"You mentioned a laptop I could use?" Alex hated the way his cheeks heated when he spoke, but he couldn't seem to shake free of the lingering embarrassment. He wasn't used to relying on anyone or asking for help, and that's all he'd been doing since he called Tristan from the hospital. It had been a moment of weakness that prompted him to do it. A flare of panic and dread had gripped him. He made the call out of desperation.

The nurse told him they'd discharge him soon and asked him kindly if he had anywhere to go. Alex went to shake his head. A sick sensation of loss and being lost churned the bile in his stomach. And then he remembered Tristan and a little of the panic eased.

Ben set the laptop on the table with the charging cord. "It's not password protected or anything. Tristan tells me you're a graphic designer?"

Alex nodded. It wasn't the only thing he did, and it wasn't what he used to do, but it paid the bills now. Most of the time.

"This might not be capable of doing everything you need it to do, but you can download whatever you need to try making it work. Or there's a desktop at the bookstore you can use. Let me know what you need."

Ben's kindness was easily given. Everything he said was matter of fact, and Alex had trouble believing he was real. No one was this perfect or this nice to their husband's ex. Husband's were jealous and possessive. Well, to be fair, Alex saw how possessive Ben was of Tristan. It wasn't overly obvious, but it was in the little things.

The way Ben talked of him. Then there was the way he looked at him, like he was always one blink away from pinning him to the wall and crashing their mouths together. The way Ben loved Tristan was obvious to anyone, but even more obvious to Alex, who knew what it was like to love someone as special as Tristan. The way Ben loved Tristan made it easy for Alex to like him.

Ben offered to make Alex breakfast, but didn't argue when Alex turned him down. He did, however, insist that Alex was welcome in their home and that he could eat and use whatever he wanted. Then, thankfully, Ben left with a promise to be back in a few hours once Maggie's shift started. Alex told him not to hurry back, and he meant it.

When the front door clicked shut, Alex breathed a sigh of relief and sat down on the couch. He hadn't been truly alone since the fire, and the sudden silence of Ben and Tristan's house made Alex's skin crawl. He felt like an intruder rather than a guest.

Alex pushed himself to his feet and plugged the laptop in at the kitchen table. He drank the rest of his cold coffee and sat down to catch up on his emails. It took his mind off things for a while. He poked around the computer and it would be basically useless for design, he'd still be able to code and build websites for his clients.

He raked a hand through his hair. It was getting too long, and the ends tickled at the tops of Alex's ears, but he didn't hate it. Alex shook a knot of tension out of his shoulders and tried to refocus on setting up a website for a client. The shrill ring of a phone snapped Alex out of his shaky concentration.

He got up and padded to the living room and stared at the phone for a beat before plucking it off the cradle. He hit talk and pressed the phone to his ear. "Stuart residence."

"Hey, I hope I didn't wake you." Tristan's chipper voice made it impossible for Alex to keep a smile at bay.

"I've been up for a while getting some work done."

"I got a text that the stuff I ordered for you is on the way. I wanted to let you know so you can get it off the porch when it gets there. I usually have stuff delivered to the bookstore because of porch pirates, but I wanted you to have some things as soon as possible."

"You're rambling." Alex leaned against the door frame.

Tristan exhaled. "Sorry. It's been a hell of a day. I was at the hospital, but I didn't get a chance to ask about your neighbor yet. I'll find out before the end of my shift."

Alex was about to tell Tristan that it was okay, to not worry about it because Tristan had already done so much for him, but the crackle of a radio and a voice in the background signaled the end of their conversation.

"Shit. We got a call. I have to go. See you at home." Tristan ended the call and Alex let the phone linger at his ear, listening to the dead air. He hung it up and went back to the computer, but he couldn't concentrate.

Alex turned the computer off and gave himself a tour of the house. He didn't go into the master bedroom, but he did peak into it, admiring the king sized bed and the rumpled covers. He turned away and walked back down the hallway, admiring the photos they'd hung.

A timeline of their relationship hung on the wall. Tristan and Ben at a fair, laughing, feeding each other cotton candy. Tristan on Ben's back, kissing his cheek. Tristan and Ben in the water. Tristan and Ben and a third guy. Alex remembered Tristan mentioning him a time or two, but the details were hazy. He'd been with Ben and Tristan for a while, from what Alex could remember.

Alex stared at the wedding photo for longer than he meant to, but Tristan and Ben were an amazing-looking couple, and though Alex had seen some of their wedding photos on social media, this one hadn't been up there. In the photo, they were almost kissing. Ben's left hand, the wedding ring shining bright on his finger, cupped Tristan's cheek. Their eyes were locked and the expressions on their faces conveyed the bottomless pit of adoration they felt for each other.

Alex felt like a voyeur staring at the photo, but he couldn't tear his eyes away, not until a brief knock at the door got his attention. As promised, a couple of boxes sat on the porch and a delivery vehicle backed out of the driveway and onto the street.

Alex took the boxes into the kitchen and set them down at the table. He retrieved a knife from the knife block on the counter and carefully opened the boxes.

Shirts. Shoes. Underwear. Pants. Socks. A toothbrush. Some toiletries. A jacket. Tristan had done too much, but Alex couldn't say anything but thank you. He could never repay Tristan for his kindnesses. Even if Tristan would let him, Alex knew Tristan didn't want to be repaid. Not in cash. He'd want Alex to put his life back together. He'd barter boxer briefs and a bed at night for Alex to find his footing, for Alex's happiness.

Alex put the clothing in the wash and pulled his other clothes on. He washed Ben's borrowed sweats with his new things and broke the boxes down. He tucked them away in the laundry room where he spotted a recycling bin.

Unable to concentrate, Alex curled up on the couch and turned the tv on. He found a local news station and waited for coverage about the fire. He didn't have to wait long, but what he saw made his stomach turn.

The fire leveled the building. The news anchor stood in front of a pile of steaming rubble. Broken beams smoldered in a close-up shot. The only thing that survived were the concrete steps going up to where the front doors used to stand. The building had collapsed in on itself and had continued to burn. Heat from the fire melted the siding of the building near it, but the fire department had contained the blaze and had prevented other property damage.

No lives were lost. Alex turned the tv off and raked shaking a hand down his face. He knew it wasn't possible, but he thought he could smell the thick, black smoke. The heat from the flames in the stairwell had been almost unbearable, and he'd had to half carry George down the final flight when the heat and the smoke had become too much for him.

Alex had basically collapsed into the arms of a fireman, which sounded a lot sexier than the reality. The reality of it had been terrifying. Alex had thought he and George might die in that stairwell. Once outside, the sudden burst of fresh air made them both cough harder.

Someone helped Alex away from the building and sat him down. They strapped an oxygen mask to his face and wrapped a blanket around him, and everything between that and Tristan showing up at the hospital was a blur of flames and faces. Questions came at him from all sides and he must have answered them, because the faces never stopped talking to him and fussing with him.

Alex curled up on the couch and stared at the blank television until he was sure he saw flames dance in the dark screen. He didn't sleep. He couldn't. Not when his brain kept shouting at him, telling him over and over how lucky he was. But... Alex didn't feel lucky. He knew he should be grateful he wasn't hurt, but it was hard to be happy when everything he had was a pile of stinking ashes.

7

BEN

Alex had been with them for two weeks and it dawned on Ben that Alex had barely left the house since they'd brought him home from the hospital. Alex didn't have a car, but they'd given him a spare key and told him he was free to come and go as he pleased.

So far, Alex stayed close to the house. He spent as much time as he could on the computer coding and working for clients. He'd get off to eat dinner with Ben and Tristan, but often Tristan would try to get Alex to sit down after with them, and Alex wouldn't.

Ben wanted to get Alex out of the house for a while. It couldn't be good for someone to spend all their time in one place. Ben liked home as much as the next person, but he enjoyed going out, too. He liked working at the bookstore and talking to the customers.

"Alex, how about your bring the laptop down to the bookstore today?" Alex lifted his head from the project he currently tapped away on. It all looked foreign to Ben. It might as well have been written in alien, but Alex clearly knew what he was doing.

"I don't want to be in your way."

"You won't be. There's free Wi-Fi at the bookstore and there's a couple bistro tables set up in the front by the windows. I thought it might be nice for you to have a change of scenery. While you're there, you can have a look at the desktop and see if you can use it for your other work. I know the laptop is older and doesn't suit all your needs the way you need them too."

Alex hesitated, like the thought of another day all by himself wasn't a big deal.

"Come on, put your jacket on. Let's go."

Alex set his jaw defiantly. "I'm fine here. Thanks."

Ben grit his teeth, then licked his lip and took a breath. "You can't stay cooped up here all the time. It'll do you some good to get out and be around people. And you should take a look at the computer, see if you can make it work for you."

Alex glowered, but Ben held firm.

"We can stop on the way home and grab Dim Sum."

Mentioning Tristan's favorite made Alex's shoulders relax, and he considered the offer for only a moment before he gave a tight nod, signaling his resignation. Ben waited while Alex packed up the laptop and slipped into his jacket and his shoes.

They climbed into the car and Alex seemed happy to not speak on the short drive to the bookstore.

Ben unlocked the door and waited until Alex was inside before he relocked it and killed the security system. "This place was my uncle's. When he died, I inherited the house and the bookstore." Ben offered that tidbit of information to Alex. Alex tilted his head, indicating interest, and Ben forged forward. He leaned against the counter and Alex put the computer down.

"Before I moved here, I lived in Seattle. I was the only one in my family who had anything to do with Uncle Phil. See, Uncle Phil was gay like me, and our families, while tolerant, were only barely tolerant. The kind of acceptance you get if you toe the line. You could be out, but not too out. You could be gay, but not too gay."

"Sounds like my family." Alex offered Ben a smile of support.

Ben took a breath and steadied himself. It had been a while since he talked about his past like this. It was a story Tristan knew well, but Tristan thankfully couldn't relate to Ben's struggle with his family. Whereas they tolerated Ben, Tristan was celebrated. The baby boy of the family had been loved before he came out and adored after.

But Ben saw a flicker of recognition and bone deep understanding in Alex's eyes when he spoke of his family and that made him open his mouth and keep going. "Uncle Phil dying saved me. I had nothing in Seattle. A shitty apartment. A family who sent a yearly obligatory invite to join them for Christmas. I maxed out my credit card for the flight to get here, and I stepped into the little corner of the world Uncle Phil had carved out for himself. I think, sometimes, that he saved my life with this, you know." Ben pushed off the counter and looked around the store that had become a second home to him. "Sometimes you don't realize how much help you need until it's given."

Before Alex could linger too long on his words, Ben motioned to the back. "Follow me, I'll show you around."

By the time the store opened, Alex busied himself in the office. The computer had been more than good enough for him to get some of his other programs going on it so he could get back to doing other work.

During a lull in customers, Ben's cell phone rang, and he answered a call from his husband. "Hey you, how's your day?" Ben answered. He bent at the waist and put his elbows on the counter.

"I called the house, but Alex isn't answering. I'm worried about him."

"Shit. I'm sorry, love. It's fine. He's here with me. It was a spur-of-the-moment thing."

Tristan exhaled. "Well, I feel dumb." A weak laugh filled Ben's ear. "I was about to flip the lights on and go home to check on him."

"He's been working his ass off day and night."

"I've tried getting him to take a break, but he won't. He's determined."

Ben thought Alex might also be using work as an excuse to hide from things he didn't want to face, but he kept that opinion to himself for now. A couple of guys came in and made their way down the far wall where Ben kept a healthy stock of LGBT+ romance.

"Maybe we can persuade him to watch a movie with us tonight." Ben suggested.

"He's more of a video game guy." Tristan said, then blurted. "Oh, my god. That's it. I'll dust the consoles off tonight."

Ben grinned. "You'll finally have someone else to beat in Mario Kart."

Tristan laughed. "I'll wipe the floor with both of you. Tell Alex it's on."

Their conversation ended when Tristan got a call. Ben wanted to go into the back and check on Alex, but customers kept him glued to the front until Maggie showed up for her shift.

Ben greeted her, then slipped into the back. Alex was so engrossed in his work that he didn't hear Ben come in.

"Hey, you."

Alex jumped, then grinned as if he were smiling at his own foolishness. Ben didn't think he'd seen Alex smile before, and though it happened faster than a lightning strike, the sight had been arresting.

"How's it going?"

Alex stretched and rolled his head in semi circles. "Good. Better now that I've been able to finish up a few things and send invoices. Get some money coming in so I can get a new computer and find a place to live."

"You know Tristan and I love having you."

Alex raised an eyebrow. "You love having your husband's ex live in your spare room?"

Ben smiled at Alex's skepticism. He crossed his arms in front of himself and stared Alex down. "Why wouldn't I? Tristan and I are solid. You're his friend. Being there for you makes him happy, which makes me happy. Besides, I'm not a monster. I'm glad we can help you."

Alex leaned back and examined Ben's face for a moment. "You're serious?"

"You doubt me?" When Alex didn't answer right away, Ben added, "Do you doubt Tristan?"

"No." Alex exhaled. "He's as honest as they come."

"Then stop hiding from him." Ben took a step forward. "He's worried about you. He wants to be your friend. Let him."

"I'm fine."

"Good." Ben gave Alex a bright smile. "Then you'll play Mario Kart with us tonight?"

Alex scoffed. "You mean, I'll let Tristan kick my ass? The man is a demon."

"I know. He's never lost against me. I'm not much of a challenge."

"Maybe we can team up and beat him together. Two against one might even the odds."

"I like the way you think. Come on, let's walk down the block for coffee."

"I have..." Alex stretched, a grimace crossed his face.

Ben cut him off. "A thing to finish. Yeah. I know. And it will be here when we get back in ten minutes. And your back will thank you."

Ben watched Alex's expression. For a moment he looked like he wanted to defy Ben, dig his heels in and be difficult, but like this morning, Alex acquiesced. He shrugged into his jacket and leveled a look at Ben.

"You're bossy, you know that?"

"You could always stay here." Ben said, though, it was a lie. Alex had been isolating himself, and Ben hated to see it. Not only did it hurt Tristan to see his friend curl into himself, but Ben wanted more for Alex, too. He barely knew him, but that didn't matter to Ben. Alex was important to Tristan, so he was important to Ben. it was that simple, and that complicated. Because now Ben wanted Alex to be happy, because no one should look as sad as Alex looked.

After a quick introduction to Maggie, they walked out into the fresh air. Ben's bookstore was in a quiet neighborhood. Most of his customers were foot traffic from the nearby college and the shopping mall a block over.

"How d'you meet Tristan?" Alex asked.

"He hasn't told you?"

Alex shrugged.

"I had an employee pass out at work once. I was new to town, didn't know anybody, barely knew my employees name. It was the second day we were open. I called an ambulance, even though Trevor insisted he was fine."

"And in swooped Tristan."

"He ended up being more concerned about me than Trevor. Trevor had recovered fine, but between my unchecked grief, moving across the country, and opening a bookstore, Trevor's incident was icing on the cake. I had my very first panic attack right there on the floor of the shop."

They reached the cafe Ben liked to frequent, and he pulled the door open and ushered Alex in ahead of him. Ben's favorite barista greeted them and he ordered a French vanilla cappuccino. Alex did the same. Ben bought a chocolate chip cookie the size of a sandwich plate for Maggie and they headed back down the block.

"So he came into the store and talked you down from a panic attack, and you lived happily ever after?"

"That's the g-rated version." Ben glanced at Alex and his grin died when he saw the look on Alex's face.

Melancholy opened up to desolation, and they both folded in on themselves to reveal nothing but a smooth poker face. "I'm glad he found someone again. I'm glad he's happy."

"He will be until we kick his ass in Mario Kart later." When Alex smiled at Ben, it made him feel like he'd won something. He decided to enjoy the small victory even when Alex locked himself away in the office until Ben collected him when it was time to leave.

Whatever somber state Ben might have put Alex in earlier, the promise of dinner and video games had put them both in good moods. Ben ordered far too much food as a result, but he didn't care because Alex smiled again when Ben told him he'd gone behind his back and found out what his favorites were from Tristan.

Alex accused him of not playing fair, but Ben shrugged his comment off. It wasn't about being fair; he wanted to tell Alex. It wasn't even about Tristan at this point. Alex needed a friend, Ben had come to realize over the past couple weeks, and he was feeling like he could be that friend.

8

TRISTAN

"Who shot that blue shell?" Tristan squawked. He stuck his tongue out the side of his mouth and leaned into his turn. He knew it didn't help him steer, but with two against one he had to try? Next to him, Ben laughed and bumped into his shoulder. "You're only in the lead because you're cheating," Tristan complained.

Alex laughed as he crossed the finish line after Ben, leaving Tristan eating their dirt in last place.

"Tristan loses again." Alex set his controller down and leaned back. "What's that, four games in a row?"

"I was going easy on you." Tristan went to the main menu and selected a different track. It was loser's choice, after all.

"Going easy on us?" Ben laughed. "That's an interesting way to say you're getting your ass kicked."

Tristan didn't mind losing. Especially when sandwiched between Ben and Alex on the couch. He knew logically that Ben hadn't known Alex before, but it still felt like old times to Tristan. Takeout and a beer, followed by a few rounds of video games and laughter. It made the nostalgia in Tristan flare up and he basked in the glow.

It wasn't old times, but it was better. He had Ben, and their love, and their life. Which he adored. Not that something had been missing, but Tristan hadn't known how much he'd missed having Alex around until recently. And a small selfish part of him didn't want Alex to leave. It was like having the best parts of his twenties, and the best part of his present, all wrapped up in one too-good-to-be-true package.

But Tristan couldn't expect Alex to stay longer than he had to, and he couldn't expect Ben to let him. As it was, Ben was a godsend of a man. It was a rare person who would not only befriend, but house their husband's ex.

In his head, Tristan blamed his distracting thought process for his subsequent loss. Out loud, however, he blamed Ben and Alex. "You two are dirty rotten cheaters." Tristan put his controller down and stood up. "I'm going to need another beer if I'm going to survive the two of you. Do you want another one, babe?"

"No, thanks." Alex said at the same time as Ben.

Tristan turned around and Ben stared at him, mouth agape. Alex flushed and stood up. "Uh. Shit, sorry. No, I'm good. I'm going to, um… go."

"You don't have to go." Ben tried telling Alex, but he was already down the hallway, retreating from them.

"Are you sure you don't want that beer?" Tristan asked as he went to the fridge and retrieved a cold one. He cracked it open and went back to the couch. He sat next to Ben and nestled in against his side. "Are you mad?"

"No," Ben's answer was quick, and he plucked the beer from Tristan's hand and took a sip before passing it back. "I'm not mad."

"How are you okay with this?" Tristan asked. "You're like the unicorn of husbands."

Ben took a moment to answer. "I love you, and I trust you."

Tristan took a sip of beer and passed the can back to Ben. "I know that, but there's got to be more to it than that?"

"Why? Love and trust? Are they not enough? Do I get jealous when I think of you and Alex and the fact that you used to be together? That you have a history with him? Yes, but jealousy is... well, we've been over this when we were with Eric. Jealousy is an okay emotion to have, it's what you do with it that matters. But I'm not even jealous."

"Okay. So, you're okay with it because you love and trust me, and you're not jealous. Not even a little?"

Ben kissed the side of Tristan's head. "Not even a little. Besides, what good does jealousy do? If I were jealous, I'd come talk to you about it, and we'd work through it like we always do."

"I don't want you to do things you're not on board with." Tristan dropped his voice to a whisper. "I know you do a lot of things for me because you love me, but I don't want you to do things you're not okay with, just to make me happy."

Ben cupped Tristan's cheek and turned his head toward him. He pressed a kiss against Tristan's lips. Firm, but not hard. His tongue snaked inside Tristan's mouth, opening him. The kiss tasted like beer. Tristan wanted Ben to push him to the floor and use him. But they had a guest and Tristan couldn't imagine fucking in the living room with a guest in the house.

Ben pulled away. "Someone's hungry." He swiped his thumb along Tristan's lower lip.

Tristan whimpered. He was starving for Ben to touch him with force and ferocity and love and adoration. "Please."

"We have a guest." Ben stated. But it wasn't a no. He dipped his thumb between Tristan's lips. Tristan sucked on the digit, watching the way Ben's nostrils flared. "Can you be quiet?"

Tristan nodded.

"Then get to bed and get ready. I'll clean up and be right there." Ben removed his thumb from Tristan's mouth and swatted Tristan's ass when he stood.

Tristan hurried down the hallway and into his bedroom. He tried not to look at the door of the spare room or think about the person behind it, but Alex was on his mind. If for no other reason than it made Tristan determined to be as quiet as he could.

He stripped naked and got the lube from the bedside table. He knelt on the bed and set it next to him. Tristan thought maybe he should've gone after Alex, but maybe he shouldn't have. Would Alex have wanted to be assured his slip up was okay, that no harm would come from it? Or would he want to be left alone? Tristan wasn't sure. In the moment he'd been concerned about Ben's feelings about Alex's slip, but now Tristan wondered if he should've been more concerned about Alex.

"I can hear you thinking from across the room." Ben's presence startled Tristan. Ben approached slowly. Tristan heard the clink of his belt buckle and the whoosh of fabric as he pulled his pants off. "No thinking. Lay on your stomach. Spread your legs for me."

Tristan lowered himself down and stretched out like a starfish. His face was half buried in the thick comforter and he closed his eyes. Tristan waited for an endless moment until Ben finally climbed onto the bed. He positioned himself between Tristan's spread legs and gripped both Tristan's cheeks in his hands. He spread them and made a quiet, pleased sound.

Tristan wiggled his butt, and Ben dug his fingers into the meaty flesh. "Behave."

Tristan's cock was trapped between his body and the bed, or it would have twitched at the tone of voice Ben used. Tristan loved it when Ben ordered him around. He loved Ben in all his forms. Bossy and forceful or sweet and attentive, and suddenly Tristan wondered what Ben would be like with Alex.

Ben stroked his hands up Tristan's back. "You're still thinking. Maybe I should stretch you out until I can fit my fist in your ass, really give you something to think about."

Tristan whimpered. He loved the process of being fisted. The slow stretch and endless use of lube. The growing feeling of fullness and the moments when it all seemed too much, too big, like he'd die if Ben stuck his hand inside him all the way.

But Tristan couldn't be quiet for that. There was no way. He whimpered again, burying the sound in the comforter.

"No? You don't want my hand inside you? Stretching you? Fucking you?"

"He'll hear."

Ben's weight shifted, and Tristan heard the distinct squelch of the lube bottle. It echoed in the quiet room and Tristan laughed into the bed. He turned his head to look over his shoulder at Ben. "I bet he heard that."

Ben shrugged, nonplussed, and reached down to stroke the lube over his cock. Almost as good as getting to touch Ben, was watching Ben touch himself, and Tristan twisted his body to get a better look.

"I'm sure he's heard people have sex before." Ben offered logic, but Tristan's brain didn't want to accept it. Of course Alex had heard people have sex before. They'd watched people fuck when they were together. It shouldn't bother him, but that was a lifetime ago and Tristan had trouble keeping Alex off his mind when he was across the hall.

Ben looked down at Tristan, and a slow smile spread across his face. "Don't worry, I'll help you be quiet. Now relax."

Tristan let his body go limp and he relaxed back into the mattress. With no prep, just a cock covered in lube, Ben pressed against Tristan's entrance.

"Deep breath, babe, that's it." Ben coaxed Tristan as though it was his first time having sex.

The thought struck Tristan, and he rolled with it. "Be gentle." He whispered. "It's my first time." He felt foolish, but then Ben's hands caressed Tristan's back again.

"Don't worry, I'll make it good for you." Ben pressed forward and the head of his cock breached Tristan's ass. "So good, baby. You're sexy like this."

Tristan bit back a whimper and Ben rewarded him by sliding in further. The stretch made Tristan pant into the bed. "Oh my god," Tristan whispered.

Ben's weight shifted. "Close your legs."

"Like this?" Tristan obeyed, pretending to be hesitant.

"Yeah, like that. Fuck, that's good."

Tristan's stomach fluttered at Ben's praise. He must have made a sound because Ben lowered himself down over top of Tristan. Ben slid a hand under Tristan, then covered his mouth. Ben's breath was hot in Tristan's ear. His voice was low and gravelly, sex-filled and hot as hell.

"You're going to be quiet for me, right, sweetheart?"

Tristan nodded, he tried to arch his spine to take Ben deeper. Ben moaned in his ear.

"Be still, baby. Trust me to take care of you. I promise it won't hurt. I know you're nervous, but I've got you."

Tristan whimpered into Ben's hand. He was fucking desperate for Ben's cock, he might explode with the waiting, but then Ben's hand tightened over Tristan's face and he pressed inside him. He moved slow and gentle, like he really was fucking a virgin. The roar of blood rushing through Tristan's body and the weight of Ben on top of him, pinning him down, drowned out everything else.

Ben's voice was rough in Tristan's ear as he thrust inside him, his pace increasing. His whisper tugged at Tristan's cock. "Look how amazing you're doing. I told you I'd be gentle."

Tristan groaned and Ben's hand tightened on his face. "Hush now. You have to be quiet or people will hear you."

Tristan whimpered. He couldn't help it, not with Ben pinning him down, holding him still, fucking him, silencing him, surrounding him. It was too good. Too much. Too big. Too hot. Tristan whimpered again, desperate for Ben to fuck him harder.

"Hush now. It's okay. I've got you." Ben whispered in Tristan's ear and he thrust inside him, hard and deep and delicious. Tristan moaned into Ben's hand. Ben had eased his grip a little, but tightened it again when he increased his pace.

Ben set a furious pace, sliding in and out of Tristan. His hips snapped and Tristan heard flesh hitting flesh over Ben's heavy breaths. Lost in the sensations, for a moment he didn't realize Ben was finishing, not until his erratic thrusts slowed.

Ben didn't leave Tristan hanging for long. He pulled out and rolled Tristan over onto his back. His mouth crashed down against Tristan's, hungrily consuming him. He wrapped his hand around Tristan's poor, neglected cock and gave it a tug.

Tristan wrapped his arms around Ben and pulled him closer. He thrust his tongue in Ben's mouth and let Ben drown out his desperate moans as he careened toward the edge.

Ben brought Tristan to the edge, then kissed him as he tumbled over it, spilling into Ben's skillful hand. Ben kissed him until they were quiet, then he brought his sticky hand to Tristan's mouth and Tristan's greedy tongue poked out and he cleaned his release from Ben's hand.

"How d'you enjoy your first time? Did I hurt you?" Ben asked, a hint of humor made the corners of his eyes crinkle.

Tristan burrowed himself against Ben and closed his eyes. "Never."

9

ALEX

Alex might have tried to distract himself with work, but there was no way he could think straight. How could he have been so stupid? Of course Tristan hadn't been talking to him. He hadn't called him a sweet pet name, but Alex had answered as though he had. As though the hands of time had turned back and things were the way they used to be.

He didn't think Ben would be mad; he didn't seem to be the type, but Alex's absolute humiliation kept him locked away in his room. He really needed to get his own place.

The sound of their bedroom door closing got Alex's attention briefly, but he soon got lost in his head again. Thinking of how he could afford to get a new computer and get an apartment and move out.

Alex didn't have the luxury of a support system like Tristan did. It was just him now, and he was tired. Tired of chasing clients to get paid. Tired of working twelve hours a day in front of a computer. He didn't hate his job, but it was hard to like anything when everything seemed bleak.

A sound from across the hall got Alex's attention. A quiet moan. Then nothing. The sound of voices, muffled and murmuring. Alex forced himself to stay put. He didn't need to go to his door and press his ear against the wood. He knew what was happening across the hall.

Alex bit his lip and his hand traveled to his neglected cock. It twitched to life and lay suddenly half-hard, trapped against his leg. He pulled it out and gave it a cursory stroke, straining in case another sound filtered across the hallway.

Guilt made his face flush, but Alex didn't stop touching himself. He couldn't. He'd realized how fucking long it had been since he'd enjoyed himself this way. The fire had thrown him for a loop, and before that he'd stopped looking for hookups and had settled for jacking off in the shower, because that's what he was used to. Pleasure had become routine until it lost meaning.

Alex spit in his hand, spread his legs a little and reached down with both hands now, one tugging at his cock, the other stroked his balls. He closed his eyes and tried not to think of anything but the moment. He concentrated on the sensation of skin on skin, of precum oozing out of his cock, easing the slide of his hand up and down the shaft.

Alex kept his lips pressed together. Jerking off to the thought of Tristan getting fucked wasn't something nice house guests did. Especially considering Tristan was his ex, it made it extra wrong for him to even entertain the thought.

But he did. He stroked his dick, basking in the feel of the weight in his hand. He couldn't remember the last time he'd been this hard. Across the hall, Tristan was getting fucked. The years had been kind to Tristan, who was still as beautiful as ever. He could see him, bent over the edge of the bed, hands on his ass to pull himself open. Alex would run his fingers down his crease and press them into his tight little hole, and he'd moan around Ben's cock. Because suddenly Alex couldn't separate the two in his head.

They had married and Alex had no place between them. He was on the outside, looking in. Except this was a fantasy, and he could do whatever he wanted. In his fantasy he fucked Tristan, pushed himself deep into his hole, and he grabbed Ben. They'd kiss like it was a battle, and he'd let Ben win, because he'd already won. Tristan was his, and even in his fantasy, Alex couldn't make himself think of Tristan any other way.

Tristan didn't belong to him, but that didn't stop Alex from wishing he could spread his cheeks and taste the salt of his skin. It didn't make the thoughts of sliding deep inside him, or kissing the curve of his neck, or the thought of burying his face in Tristan's crotch go away.

Tristan was off limits, but Alex stroked his cock, anyway. He'd let himself have this one indulgence. This one sinful action. He'd allow himself a few minutes of lust to chase the darkness and the numbness away.

Alex bit back a groan and jerked his hand faster. He tugged on his balls and they throbbed in his hand, hot and tight and full. His breath came in ragged gasps as his lips fell open and he finished, Tristan's image in his mind, his name on his tongue.

Alex's shirt got the worst of his cum shot. He tugged it off and used it to clean his hand. He didn't want to risk going out into the hallway to use the bathroom in case Tristan and Ben were still fucking, or had finished and had guessed what Alex had been up to.

In the aftermath of his orgasm, the mistake he'd made was suddenly a grievous error instead of the small faux pax he'd told himself it was a minute ago. He felt stupid, because now he'd have to face Tristan and Ben after he'd fantasized about fucking his ex and his husband.

The idiocy of his decision sat in his belly like a ton of bricks. He scrubbed his non-cum hand down his face, then flipped on his stomach and buried his face into his pillow.

Before guilt could settle in deeper, he slept.

The morning came too soon, and with it the knowledge of what he'd done. He wore his secret like a weight in his bones. It was Sunday. The bookstore was closed and Tristan had the day off. Alex tried to keep track of their schedules so he could make himself as scarce as possible when they weren't working.

Alex walked into the kitchen, because he couldn't hide forever, and poured himself a cup of coffee then emptied the dishwasher while he sipped at it. He'd taken to doing a bit of the house work while he'd been staying.

Tristan came into the kitchen wearing a shirt and a pair of tight jeans with rips all down the front. "Hey, I was hoping you'd be awake."

"You were?" Alex wrinkled his brow and silently prayed that Tristan wouldn't mention his stupid mistake last night. Well, the one he knew about.

"Ben and I are going out to my folk's house for lunch, and Mom wants me to bring you."

Tristan's mom was a goddess. She was soft and sweet and warm, like a fairy godmother from a bedtime story.

Tristan took Alex's shock for hesitation. "She insists. Which means she'll be sad if you don't come."

"That's dirty, Tris." Alex frowned and sipped at his coffee. He couldn't go to Tristan's family home. He couldn't sit there knowing that he'd made Tristan choose all those years ago, and he'd lost. Especially because Tristan clearly didn't regret his decision. Not that he should. Or that Alex wanted him too, not really.

"Come on. Mom's making your favorite. Are you really not going to show up?"

"I don't want to intrude."

"You can't intrude on something you're invited to." Tristan rolled his eyes and stalked over to the coffeepot. "You're so difficult sometimes. Just come to Mom and Dad's with us." Tristan turned his head when Ben entered the room. Alex watched their gazes meet from across the room. "Tell him, Ben."

"Bonnie invited you specifically."

Alex bit his lip. He wanted to argue, but it was two against one, three if you included Tristan's mom, who seemed to have a vote even though she wasn't present. Alex let his gaze drift to Ben, who stood there unaffected by Alex's presence in their lives.

Because he didn't know Alex had jerked off thinking about the two of them.

"Go get dressed, Alex." Ben said with an air of finality that made the hairs on the back of Alex's neck stand on end.

Alex, for a moment, was speechless. More of a gaping fish, mouth hanging open, lips moving without sound, than he was a person. Then he bristled and snapped his mouth shut.

"I'm not sure I want to go." Alex said, purposely ignoring how wrong those words sounded on his tongue. He folded his arms over his chest and pulled his shoulders back. Defiantly, he stared at Ben. Tension in the room thickened as Alex felt Tristan's gaze on him.

Tristan didn't say a word, though. He stood there silently. Like he'd been silent the night before. Nearly silent, anyway. Alex tried not to flinch at the thought. It was wildly inappropriate to be thinking of Ben fucking Tristan. The knowledge of what he'd done made the thought worse.

Alex's face heated, and his traitorous cock thickened. The tension in the room and the embarrassment of what he'd done had his body confused. His adrenaline spiked as though he were gearing up for an argument, but his cock twitched in expectation of inappropriate jerk-off session number two.

Alex wanted to thrust his tongue out at Ben and proclaim that he wasn't the boss of him, but that felt exceedingly juvenile.

"Come on, you heard Tristan. His family invited you. They want you there."

But did Ben? Alex squirmed, uncomfortable with the idea that he wanted Ben to want him there. But if Ben wanted him there, that meant he wasn't an intruder, an interloper, an unwelcome house guest taken in out of pity and a sense of obligation to please his husband.

Ben rolled his eyes. "You have ten minutes to get dressed, or I'll drag you out of the house in your sweats."

Alex scowled and left the room. He wasn't running away, but Ben had called his attention to Alex's sweats, and if Tristan or Ben happened to glance down, they'd see the erection he was sporting. No, Alex wasn't giving in. But once he was in his room, he stripped out of his sweats and into a pair of jeans and a Henley. It didn't surprise Alex that everything had fit him perfectly. Tristan knew his sizes and was better at the whole picking clothes that looked nice together thing. Alex was happy if his clothes were clean. Hell, if he could get away with it, he'd wear cargo pants, but Tristan would tease him mercilessly.

Alex grumbled under his breath and yanked a pair of socks on. He stopped in the bathroom to clean up a bit and took a deep breath before he dared to go back out into the main room where Ben and Tristan were.

Alex knew he was living under their roof, but Ben couldn't boss him around. He shouldn't secretly like that Ben hadn't given him a choice, but it took some responsibility off his shoulders. If he went and things were awkward and terrible, as they likely would be, Alex could blame Ben. After all, it wasn't as though Alex wanted to go.

"That color looks good on you."

Alex turned around and faced Tristan, whose eyes raked up and down Alex's body. The attention made Alex shift his weight from one foot to the other. "Thanks," he managed after a minute.

"If you don't want to come, Ben can't make you."

Alex nodded. Logically, he knew that. But Alex wanted to go. He wanted to get out of the house and talk to people, and Tristan's family had always been amazing. He hadn't kept in touch after the breakup, but he should have. Bonnie had been like a mother to him.

Thankfully, Ben chose that moment to come out of the bedroom, breaking up Alex's thought process with the way his jeans hugged his legs and the dress shirt, untucked with rolled-up sleeves, that made him look casually sexy in a put together way.

Fuck, Alex had to get laid. He couldn't believe he'd gone from jacking off thinking of Tristan getting fucked by Ben, to checking Ben out.

Ben looked at Alex and gave him a nod of approval. That simple nod shouldn't have zinged straight to his balls or filled his heart with joy, either. Clearly, Alex needed to get out more. He needed to get laid, or drunk, or drunk and laid. Something to get the image of Ben and Tristan out of his head before he said or did something stupid.

10

BEN

Alex insisted on making a stop on the way to Tristan's parent's house and the minute Alex was out of the car and out of earshot, Tristan turned to him.

"Did we do the right thing, making him come? I don't think he's very comfortable."

"I know I don't know him as well as you, but he seems lost."

"You always were a sucker for the lost boys." Tristan put his hand on Ben's thigh and Ben laced their fingers together.

"You were never lost."

"Eric was." Tristan's expression was still a little sad when they talked about Eric. Eric was a wound that had closed, but the scar remained, reminding them of what they'd lost.

"Alex isn't Eric," Ben stated. It was the truth. Eric had been a part of their relationship in ways Alex wasn't. But not since Eric left had anyone occupied the spare room. It had been their extra space for when they needed a break to having three to a bed for a night. "We should have seen it coming, with Eric. He was reluctant about a lot of things. I thought he'd acclimate to us over time, but..."

"It's not your fault." Tristan squeezed his hand. "If we ever find another person, we'll talk about things better than we did with Eric. We'll make it work. Though..." Tristan bit his lip. "I don't know when we'll get an opportunity to meet someone right now. It would be weird to bring someone home with Alex there, you know? Are you disappointed?"

"Never." Ben leaned across the seat and kissed Tristan. The back door opened and Alex climbed in carrying a bouquet of flowers. Ben gave Tristan a look he hoped conveyed the sincerity of his words, then turned to Alex and grinned. "You're making me look bad."

"They can be from all of us." Alex offered, setting the flowers down gently on the seat next to him. He buckled in and looked at Ben. "I don't mind."

"He was only teasing," Tristan said. "Mom will love the flowers."

Ben watched the way Tristan's eyes softened around the edges when he looked at Alex. It was a look Ben had seen before sometimes when Tristan looked at him. Sometimes he'd witnessed Tristan look at Eric like that, all soft and moony-eyed. Ben forced himself to look away before Tristan noticed him staring and he started the car.

Tristan's parents lived outside the city a few miles on a stretch of empty road lined with the odd house and endless fields, surrounded by trees. In summer, when the grass in the field was tall, it reminded him a bit of the ocean, the way the wind would cause the grass to sway and wave.

It reminded him of the difference in his upbringing. Love and acceptance had surrounded Tristan, along with beauty and nature. Ben grew up in the rainy Seattle climate with parents who loved him unconditionally until he came out. Now, they might call once a year, if they remembered. And when they did, their phone calls were short and strained. They'd ask about his partner, barely willing to say Tristan's name because doing so was an admission their son was gay and married to a man.

Tristan put his hand on Ben's leg. "Babe."

Ben glanced at him, and once Tristan had his attention, his eyes darted to the steering wheel. Ben looked at his white knuckle grip and forced himself to relax.

"Everything okay?"

Ben nodded. He didn't want to rain on Tristan's parade with talk of his own shitty family, but he didn't want him jumping to his own conclusions either. "You're lucky to have a family like yours. That's all."

Tristan's hand tightened a little, and he stroked his hand down Ben's thigh in a gesture of comfort. "I know I am. But they're your family too, now."

Ben smiled at Tristan, and he was glad Tristan didn't truly understand. Made family was wonderful. He wouldn't trade his relationships with Bonnie and Greg for anything, but that didn't mean he didn't wish he could have that sort of relationship with his own parents. Since he was a kid and it became obvious to his parents, something was different about him, he'd never fit. He felt like a needle in a haystack, as if he didn't belong, and was invisible in his own house.

He'd spent years losing himself trying to fit in until his uncle died and moving across the country ended up being the best decision he'd ever made. His family hadn't tried very hard to talk him out of it. They were almost glad to see him go, if not outwardly happy. There had been a sense of relief.

Ben remembered clearly, the feeling of lightness that had bubbled out of him when he realized he didn't have to perform for anyone anymore. He wished he'd made more of an effort to know his Uncle Phil when he was alive, but Ben tried not to think too much about that, because his uncle had left everything to him because he knew Ben. He knew in his soul what kind of hell Ben lived with, being an outsider in his own family. And he'd offered a lifeline.

Tristan's family home came into view, an old farmhouse

remodel that sat on the edge of an endless field on one side, with a copse of trees on the other. Ben remembered barbeques and holidays spent out here. Casual Sunday dinners and wedding receptions. All of Bonnie and Greg's children got married, held the service in the family's backyard.

Tristan and Ben had married in the gazebo out back, and now Ben wondered if Alex had ever sat in the gazebo with Tristan and planned a future together. The idea made Ben's stomach twist, but it hadn't worked out for them.

Ben parked the car behind Greg's SUV and climbed out. He met Tristan at the front of the car and they linked hands and walked to the door together. Ben glanced over his shoulder at Alex, who looked slightly terrified. He offered a kind smile before following Tristan up the steps.

Tristan knocked on the door and it opened to reveal Bonnie, who dried her hands on a tea towel. "How many times have I told you not to knock? It's still your house." Bonnie stepped aside and let the trio enter.

"And my mom taught me to knock first. You created a mannered monster, deal with it." Tristan toed out of his shoes and pushed them to the side with his feet, lining them up against the wall of the entryway with the other shoes.

He bent and gave her a hug. She was all of five feet tall and was thin as a reed swaying in the wind, but it would take more than a breeze to knock her over. She pulled Ben into a hug after Tristan.

"How are you? How are the books? Got anything new?"

"There's an order coming next week that will interest you." Ben said as Bonnie pulled away. He toed out of his shoes and they joined Tristan's off to the side.

"Tell me when to be there."

"You're horrible for her book addiction." Tristan said with a hint of laughter in his voice.

Bonnie playfully swatted at him. "Hush, you. And get out of

my way." She gently pushed Tristan off to the side and looked at Alex. She smiled, sweet and slow, and Ben could've sworn he saw a tear in her eye before she pulled Alex into a hug.

Tristan gripped Ben's hand and tugged him away from the scene. "Let's say hi to Dad."

Ben looked back at Bonnie and Alex. Bonnie swiped at Alex's cheek with her thumb. The pain in Alex's gaze resonated with Ben. He knew what it was like to walk into this house and be surrounded by love and not quite know what to do with it all. Ben had gotten used to it over the years, but it still threw him sometimes, the way this home felt like a real home with love and laughter and a warm acceptance Ben hadn't experienced before.

"You okay?" Tristan whispered as they entered the kitchen.

"Yeah." Ben squeezed Tristan's hand, grateful Tristan wouldn't ever know what it was like to have a family who treated him like an inconvenience. And as happy as he was for Tristan, and with Tristan, it was something he'd never understand. But Alex would, Ben thought, as he caught Bonnie's voice, sweet and low, as she talked to Alex in the entryway.

Tristan gave Ben a look that probably meant he'd want to needle him later, then let the subject drop and greeted his dad. Greg put his phone aside and pushed his glasses up the bridge of his nose.

"There're my boys. Long time no see."

Tristan looked at Ben and rolled his eyes. "Can you believe him? We were here for your birthday last month, Dad."

"How's business?" Greg asked Ben.

"Steady as always."

"Grab yourself a cup of coffee, son." Greg said to Ben.

"Do you want one, love?" Ben asked Tristan.

"No, thanks." Tristan sat at the table near his dad and they launched into family gossip mode. Ben poured a coffee for himself and tried to follow along with the conversation, but his attention drifted to Bonnie and Alex. They came into the kitchen,

Bonnie with her arm linked through Alex's. Ben couldn't help but notice the look of happiness on Bonnie's face. It reminded him of the way she looked whenever one of her kids came home.

Greg and Tristan's conversation ground to a halt and Greg got up from his chair. "Alex, how are you, son?"

Tristan's family had a habit of adopting everyone, Ben had been told. When he and his brothers were teenagers, their house was the place where everyone gathered. Everyone got folded into the flock as though they'd always belonged. It had been the same way with Ben. They'd tried with Eric, but he'd always held himself apart from Tristan's family.

Alex, however, hugged Greg then sat down across the table from him while Bonnie got him a coffee. A plate of lemon bars appeared on the table and she patted Alex on the shoulder. They had to be his favorite, Ben realized. Bonnie always made Ben an angel food cake for his birthday. For Tristan's birthday, it was strawberry cheesecake.

Alex had been away for years, but they'd tucked him back into the family and made him feel welcome. They told him they'd missed him and asked about how he was doing.

Ben knew if he went home his parents would make awkward conversation, avoiding anything too personal about his home life. They'd ask about the store and the house before they asked after Tristan. They hadn't even known about Eric. Ben had invited them to the wedding, of course, but he knew before he sent the invitation that they wouldn't come.

Tristan slipped his hand into Ben's and wound their fingers together. He gave his hand a squeeze, showing his silent support of whatever inner turmoil Ben was currently riding out. The gesture was enough to slow the roller coaster in his mind and allow him to focus on being present.

11

TRISTAN

Tristan's mom caught him alone after lunch. Ben and Alex were in the living room with his Dad and his mom followed him to the kitchen.

"Is everything okay with Ben, dear? He's quiet today."

Truthfully, Tristan didn't know what was up with his husband, and it had him worried that Alex staying with them was wearing on Ben. It had been nearly a month since the fire, but because Alex did freelance work, he struggled to get his feet under himself. Tristan knew Alex had been struggling for some time, but those were the only details he had. He should have checked in more often. Hell, even after Alex came to stay with them, Tristan hadn't pressed him for details. He didn't like prying into things that weren't his business. But Alex was living with them now, so he technically was Tristan's business.

If Ben was tiring of Alex, he'd have to leave, but Alex didn't have anywhere to go. Tristan swallowed a lump in his throat. "Everything's fine, Mom. I don't think he slept well."

"He looks troubled." Tristan's mom was a worrier, she couldn't help herself. But her anxiety fed Tristan's. Until a minute ago he'd been able to push aside the niggling feeling that something was off with Ben, but if his mom noticed then something had to be up.

"I'm sure he's just tired, Mom. Don't worry about it."

His mom frowned a little, but patted his arm. "I'll try not to, but I'm not making any promises."

Tristan returned to the living room, and he sat next to Ben. He curled into his side and Ben slung an arm around him, pulling him close. Ben brushed a kiss to the side of Tristan's head.

"Tired, babe?"

"A little." Tristan thought of his rough week. First, the car accident and the domestic dispute they had called him to. The blood didn't haunt him, nor the gore. The fractures and the lacerations didn't keep him awake at night. But the look in people's eyes when they thought they might die did. Or when they feared they might not. Those were the things that gripped tight to Tristan. They were the things he wanted to forget at the end of a long week.

"We should head home." Ben said, he gripped Tristan tighter, pulling him back to the present.

Tristan blinked and forced a smile. "I'm okay."

Tristan's dad waved him off. "Go on, get home. You look like you've been through the wringer, son. Make that husband of yours pamper you a bit."

Tristan smiled at his dad. "Ben always pampers me. I'm a lucky man."

"Let me put a plate together for you boys." Tristan's mom headed back to the kitchen.

"Mom, you don't need to do that," Tristan called after her.

"I made all these lemon bars and lord knows, I don't need to eat them." She appeared a minute later with a paper plate wrapped tight with plastic wrap. "I'd send you a Tupperware container but you never return them." She dropped the heavy hit and Tristan flushed, remembering the containers he'd brought home and set aside to return later. They were still tucked away in the cupboard somewhere.

"Sorry, Mom." Tristan stood and took the plate from her, then wrapped her in a one-armed hug. "Thanks for lunch. And lemon bars."

She patted Tristan on the back and snuck in a kiss to the cheek. "Thanks for bringing your men by."

Tristan schooled his expression at the odd choice of her words. Ben was his, but Alex was a friend. They'd been close at one time, and though they'd rekindled a sort of friendship when Alex moved back, Tristan was aware of the distance between them. A purposeful gap created by past hurts and present fears. He wondered then, what it would be like to be closer to Alex again?

Tristan shook that thought right out of his head. Or… he tried to. But it clung there as he watched Alex hug his parents goodbye, promising to keep in touch this time. He felt a little out of body when he watched Ben and Alex exchange a few words on the way to the car.

Tristan turned to his Dad, who hovered by the doorway. "You sure you're okay, son?" Worry etched his dad's expression.

"I'm tired, Dad, but I'll be fine."

His dad nodded. "Take it easy, kiddo. Love you."

"I will, Dad. Love you. Love you, Mom." Tristan gave his parents another hug then trudged to the car where Ben and Alex waited for him. He slid into the passenger seat and buckled his seat belt.

It wasn't until they were nearly home that Alex spoke. His voice came soft and unsure. "I can uh… get a hotel tonight if you two need some time together."

Tristan twisted to look at him. He furrowed his brow. "What? No. It's fine. We get plenty of time together. You don't have to leave." Tristan put his hand on Ben's leg, urging him to agree.

Alex rolled his eyes at Tristan. "You're tired, Tris. You've had a rough week. It's fine if you want some privacy to be with your husband. I know how much you value quality time."

Tristan's heart slammed against his rib cage and something got stuck in his throat. Emotions. Fear. Want. Nostalgia. Whatever it was, it felt too big for him to digest at that moment.

"I'll get a hotel."

"You're trying to get on your feet." Ben broke the awkward silence as he turned into the driveway and killed the engine. "You don't need to go anywhere. It's fine, I promise."

Tristan bristled. Ben had been firm, not with anger or annoyance, but firm like he got with Tristan sometimes.

"I wasn't saying you can't."

Alex undid his buckle and climbed out of the car. Tristan followed, and he watched Ben and Alex stand toe to toe. Ben, slightly shorter than Alex, but not by much. Not too short to look him dead in the eyes. "I'll get a hotel. Tristan needs you and I don't want to be in the way."

Ben's eyebrow ticked with the urge to arch, but Ben kept it from doing so. He licked his lips and rolled his shoulders back. He looked like he was about to speak, but then he tilted his head. "Let's finish this inside." Ben headed for the door. Tristan and Alex dutifully followed.

They stayed silent until they were safely in the living room. Then Ben turned to Alex. "Does it make you uncomfortable? The idea of you being here and maybe hearing something? Because you don't need to run off for our benefit."

Tristan turned to Alex and waited. The idea Alex might be uncomfortable never occurred to him, and guilt made him inwardly flinched when Alex sucked in a breath to answer.

"Truthfully? I don't know." Alex stood his ground, but Tristan could tell Ben's presence had an effect on Alex. Alex shifted his weight from foot to foot. He crossed his arms over his chest, then uncrossed them and tucked them in his pockets. Ben unsettled him.

Ben turned his attention to Tristan. He closed the distance between them and cradled Tristan's face in his hand. "Would it bother you?"

Tristan shivered. "Would it bother you?" He could barely get the words out through the rush of blood in his ears. The way his knees quaked made him feel weak.

"If it did, I would be asking. We can spend the night in our room... or," Ben paused.

"Or?" Tristan reached for Ben to steady himself. His fingers clung to the waist of Ben's jeans.

"Or Alex can tell me if he's comfortable and if he is, I'll spend the rest of the day taking care of you."

Tristan closed his eyes and leaned into Ben's touch. If Alex wasn't comfortable, he and Ben would go to a hotel, Tristan would beg if he had to, because he couldn't last with the noise in his head. Not without feeling like he was losing his mind.

The time it took Alex to answer stretched beyond hope, and Tristan's shoulders sagged. He truthfully didn't want to leave his home. Home made him feel safe, Ben made him feel safe. A hotel would do, but it wouldn't be the same. The sheets would smell different. The noises would be weird.

"It's... it's okay." Alex said finally.

Ben's fingers twitched against Tristan's cheek. "Go wait in the bedroom for me." Ben said before releasing him.

Tristan opened his eyes and smiled at Ben, then skirted around him and went to the bedroom as instructed. He stripped out of his clothing and stood, naked and trembling. He sucked in a deep breath and waited.

A few minutes went by before the door across the hall opened and closed and the sound of music filtered out, the bass reaching Tristan's ears. His heart pounded to the same rhythm as he waited for Ben.

Tristan shut his eyes and waited. He breathed in and out, trying to think of anything besides Alex, locked away in his room and Ben, taking his time to come for him. Making him wait. Tristan wriggled where he stood, shifting his weight impatiently. He searched for that calm place, that part of him that found comfort in the wait, but he couldn't find it.

Ben entered then, before Tristan could think too much about it. The door shut with a quiet click and Ben padded across the room, briefly fanning his fingers through Tristan's hair on the way by.

A drawer opened and shut, and Ben moved around the room again. This time he stood in front of Tristan and hooked a finger under his chin.

"Are you okay, love?" Ben asked.

Tristan trembled. He didn't know. On one hand, he wanted to say yes because he wanted to be okay. He wanted to be strong for Ben. But he couldn't, because he wasn't. He felt like a brittle leaf laying on the cold ground, waiting for the wind to blow him away, or for a shoe to crush him.

Tristan shook his head. "I don't know."

Ben stroked his hand down Tristan's face, and he cupped the side of his neck. He wrapped his fingers around the back of Tristan's neck and gripped him. The pressure grounded Tristan. He exhaled a shaky breath.

"Can you talk about it now or do you need time to gather your thoughts?"

Tristan wanted to lay himself at Ben's mercy and kiss his feet. "Please." It was the only word he could manage, but it was enough.

"Okay, love. That's okay." Ben cooed. Tristan loved the soft tone of his voice and the way it felt like silk on Tristan's tired soul. "Get up on the bed and lay face down."

Tristan did as he was told. He spread his legs because he knew that's what Ben would want.

Ben reached for Tristan and grabbed him by the ankle. Then, slowly, he massaged his way up the back of Tristan's leg, working the tired muscles with his skilled hands. Tristan moaned in the pillow.

"That's it, relax and let me take care of you."

Tristan wanted to purr, or maybe cry. Ben was good to him, good for him. He was one of the most amazing men Tristan had ever met. And yet, Tristan still felt wounded over Eric leaving. And then there was Alex. He'd thrust Ben into an awkward position, but Ben rolled with everything life threw his way and having Alex around didn't bother him.

A sharp smack to the ass had Tristan hissing.

"I said stop thinking."

"Sorry." Tristan focused on breathing, on filling his lungs and emptying them and the feeling of time slipping away. Then Ben's lubed fingers prodded at his entrance.

"Hngh." Tristan muffled his cries into the pillow as Ben slid a finger in, slowly, up to the knuckle. Tristan shook with the need to move back and fuck himself on the retreating finger, but forced himself to behave. He wanted to be good for Ben, to make him proud.

With a little gentle coaxing, Ben opened Tristan up. He fingered him until he panted and humped the mattress, then his fingers disappeared.

"Please." Tristan whined, he'd long since stopped caring how he sounded when Ben made him desperate and touch starved.

"Shhh." Ben stroked his hand down Tristan's back. "It's okay, I've got you."

Something large and blunt pressed against Tristan's hole, and he took a deep breath as Ben slid a plug inside. He winced as his hole stretched wide, then gasped when the fattest part of the plug slid in.

Tristan knew what plug it was without having seen it. It was wide, fat, uncomfortable in the best way, especially when Ben would turn the vibrator on and torture him.

Ben pressed a kiss to the base of Tristan's spine. "Now get up and put some comfortable pants on and come out to the living room."

Tristan pushed himself to his feet and his mind was blissfully quiet as he stepped shakily into a pair of zebra print pajama pants. He left the shirt off and padded out to the living room unsure of what to expect equal parts nervous about whether or not Alex would be there.

12

ALEX

Ben looked at him once Tristan had left the room. He looked as relaxed and easy going as he always did, but he definitely had a don't fuck with me glint in his eye.

"Are you uncomfortable because you don't want to see it, or because you do?" Ben asked.

"Shit." Alex breathed out. "Right for the jugular."

Ben raised an eyebrow. And waited. Well, if he was waiting for Alex to know how he felt, he'd be waiting a long fucking time. The hairs on the back of Alex's neck stood on end. He lifted a hand to rub over them, to soothe the nagging sensation that pricked his skin, but he snapped his hand back down to his side.

"I won't get in your way," Alex said. He didn't want to see this private exchange between the husbands, but he burned to see it. What did they do? How did they do it? He wondered what Ben was like when he was looking after Tristan, and how Tristan took it.

"Tristan doesn't object," Ben said simply. "Neither do I. We're grown men and for now we're sharing a space. Tristan needs something, and it's probably nothing you haven't seen before."

Alex swallowed. "Maybe that's why I should steer clear."

Ben regarded him for a long, uncomfortable moment. "Do you still have feelings for Tristan?"

Alex took a step back. "What? What kind of question is that?"

Ben shrugged. "An honest one. I don't mind if you do, but if that's the reason you're uncomfortable, I completely understand."

Alex, close to cracking, raked a hand through his hair. He couldn't look at Ben because he couldn't lie to him, but he didn't know what the truth was. Did he still have feelings for Tristan? Probably, if Alex was honest with himself. But they meant nothing. Couldn't mean anything.

Alex almost had enough money to look for his own place. His palms turned clammy at the thought of going back to living all alone, to having no one and nothing. But it was probably for the best that it happened sooner and not later, before he could fuck things up for Tristan.

"Don't," Alex grated out before he needed to clear his throat. "Don't get a hotel. Tristan wouldn't like it. If I'm not comfortable, I'll stay in my room. I have work to do, anyway."

Ben nodded, and Alex set off down the hallway. No sound came from Ben and Tristan's bedroom. Alex slipped into his room and turned some music on. He sat on his bed and let out a shaky breath. He buried his head in his hands and waited until the spinning sensation stopped.

Did he still have feelings for Tristan? Alex snorted softly. Of course he fucking did, and Ben had to have seen them written all over his face, plain as day. Alex tilted his head back, then shoved to his feet and paced in the small space.

Logically, he knew he should pack and leave. He might have, had he been able to afford it. But bills kept coming and money kept going. Alex had taken on extra clients to try to make up the difference. He had to save enough money to get out of their home. Because he did still have feelings for Tristan. He doubted that there had ever been a day when he hadn't.

With that in mind, he sat down at the borrowed laptop. His fingers hovered over the keys and he stared at the screen, but his mind wouldn't engage with his tasks. He scrubbed a hand down his face, as though he could scrub Tristan from his mind.

Call it morbid fascination, or self-flagellation, Alex wanted to see what Tristan was like now. When they were younger and had been discovering themselves together, Tristan was open and delightful. He never shied away from anything he wanted to try. His curiosity had been inspiring, and once Alex was without it, his own faded as well.

When he left, he'd left all of that behind. Instead of love, he threw himself into his career. Alex closed his eyes. Fat lot of good that did him. A recession stripped everything away from him.

He'd had a couple brief relationships in that time, both with men who were all wrong for him. His handful of friends turned out to like him better when he had nice things. And once they were gone, the friends weren't far behind.

Alex turned and stared at the door. He wondered what it would be like to walk out that door and stare his past in the face? It would be different because Tristan wasn't his and Alex wouldn't be in control anymore. Alex wanted to laugh. He'd done a shit job at being in charge of his own life and had no business pretending to be in control when he was staying in someone's spare room.

He couldn't go out there. Not with Ben knowing the truth. Because if Ben could see Alex was still half in love with Tristan, Tristan would have to know. And if he didn't already know, Alex hoped to keep his feelings hidden. He'd work harder and if he had to, he'd move into a shoebox. He'd let Tristan and Ben get back to the way their life had been before Alex crash landed in it.

It wasn't as though Alex had ever been deserving of someone like Tristan. Tristan was smart and compassionate. Gorgeous and friendly. Everyone loved him. Alex hadn't deserved him in the first place, and after his life had gone to shit, he definitely didn't deserve him.

Sick of feeling sorry for himself, Alex kept his playlist going and sat back down in front of the computer. He was supposed to be putting together a website and new branding for a local business. Instead, he googled Ben's bookstore. His online presence was dismal. An under utilized Facebook page and a yellow pages listing. No website. Nothing.

Inspired, Alex got to work. If he wanted the website to be phenomenal, he'd need better pictures, but the ones he could snag from Facebook would do for the mockup.

Alex threw himself into the project. He built a website from scratch. Along with the regular features, Alex built the bare bones of a system that would allow people to order books online directly from Ben's store. Why Ben hadn't already done it, Alex couldn't fathom.

A knock on the door drew Alex from his work. He rubbed at his eyes and looked at the clock. Hours had passed and darkness had descended outside. Alex hadn't even noticed. He pushed himself out of his chair with a groan and stretched his stiff neck as he walked to the door.

Ben stood in the hallway, arms folded over his chest. He wore a tight white shirt that stretched across his chest. Ben wasn't stacked, but he looked... good. Firm, but huggable. Alex swore internally and raised his gaze to meet Ben's.

"You need to eat."

It hadn't been a request, and Alex wasn't sure how to feel about that. "I'm fine." Alex's stomach stayed silent. Even faced with food, he likely wouldn't be able to eat in front of Ben and Tristan.

Ben stared at Alex, holding his gaze steady until Alex shifted uncomfortably.

"I said I'm fine."

"You won't see anything you don't usually see," Ben assured

him. He motioned for Alex to leave the room, expecting Alex to follow him.

Alex took a breath and tried to still his frantic pulse, but his earlier conversation with Ben had rattled him and stripped him raw. He felt terrified of what Tristan might see. Could Tristan see the feelings still lingering under the surface?

Alex slipped into the bathroom and pissed, then washed his hands. He avoided his reflection in the mirror. He didn't want to see the person he'd become. Timid and scared. Not scared, terrified. He knew the weight of regret sat heavy on his shoulders, and he didn't know how to shrug it off. One day he'd need to. And soon. He'd never deserve Tristan, but he wanted to be deserving of someone.

Alex walked out into the main living area and saw Tristan dishing up Ben. He carried the plate to him at the table, but said nothing.

"Sit down, Alex." Ben said.

Alex shifted his gaze back and forth between Ben and Tristan and reluctantly took a seat. His stomach rumbled ferociously when he caught a whiff of dinner. Alex shifted in his seat, and then Tristan brought a plate to him and set it down.

"This looks really good, Tristan."

Ben picked up his fork and dug in, keeping one eye on Tristan as he served himself and sat down.

"Thank you," Tristan said.

Nothing was different, they'd eaten together before, but the air felt sexually charged. Alex fought the urge to shift in his seat as he pushed the food around on his plate. It was simple fare; roasted chicken breast with a garden salad and a scoop of rice, buttered and salted the way Alex liked it. It made him inspect his plate further. Ranch dressing pooled on the side of his plate next to his salad instead of being drizzled on top.

Alex couldn't eat. He stared at the plate. Insignificant things like rice and dressing preferences weren't something someone should remember. Alex couldn't remember things like that about Tristan. He remembered things like the way it felt when they'd smash the snooze button and make out until the alarm went off again. The lazy way they'd linger in bed together, chasing extra minutes of quiet intimacy before the world demanded it join them. He recalled the way Tristan made him feel, alive, and safe, and whole. More than he remembered that he always ate the pickle Alex pulled out of his hamburgers.

Alex stared at his dinner. It was just food, but the side of dressing and a pat of butter had his throat closing. He couldn't do this. He couldn't read into this as much as he wanted to. Alex tightened his grip on his fork and poked a piece of cucumber. He popped it into his mouth and let the crunch of the fresh vegetable drown out his churning thoughts.

"You don't have to go back to your room, you know." Tristan sounded oddly tentative.

Alex looked at him and swallowed. "I was in the middle of a project." He thought of the bookstore's new website that sat unfinished. It was nothing more than a bare bones design with the potential to be something amazing, and he wanted to finish it as soon as possible. He owed Ben and Tristan a lot and there was no way he could ever repay them for their kindness, but he could do this small thing for them.

"Okay." Tristan gave him a sad nod and pushed at his rice instead of eating it.

Alex wanted to take his answer back. It was apparent that Tristan wanted him to stick around, but Alex could barely handle sitting at the table eating dinner with them while the air still faintly crackled with unfulfilled sexual tension.

Alex kept his eyes on his plate and finished dinner in an atmosphere that felt less like sex and more like suffocation. He'd disappointed Tristan when all the man had been asking for was his friendship. The idea of giving Tristan his friendship and nothing more had once upon a time been enough for him. He'd made decisions that lead him to a place where he'd had to learn to settle for it. It wasn't until the aftermath of the fire that Alex realized how hollow his life had been.

Being friends with Tristan should be better than nothing, but Alex ached with the need for more. What hurt the most was that Alex knew it would never be enough for him. He'd always remember with a rapier sharp longing the way Tristan had felt in his arms and in his bed. And Alex had thrown that away to chase a dream that vanished in a puff of smoke. Alex inwardly grimaced at how perfect the metaphor of things going up in flames had been for his life.

With a sour stomach and a heavy heart, Alex excused himself from the table.

"Are you okay?" Tristan asked. His voice oozed with concern Alex didn't deserve.

He made himself nod, and hoped the smile he forced didn't look too fake. "Worn out, I think."

"Okay." Tristan worried his lip between his teeth and Alex fled before he could ask whatever question it was that lingered in his gaze.

Alex flopped down into bed and almost hid under the covers like the coward he was. But he gave himself ten minutes to wallow before he got back to work on the website. Anything to distract himself from memories of Tristan's mouth on his.

13

BEN

Ben watched Alex retreat again. He was always running away from them. Ben wasn't a fool. He saw the way Alex looked at Tristan when he thought no one was looking.

Tristan stood and carried his plate to the trash, where he scraped the rest of his dinner. Ben shoved his chair out a little and patted his leg. "Come here."

Tristan shook his head a little and didn't move. Ben stood and grabbed Tristan's hand and towed him to the table, where Ben pulled him down into his lap and held him with an iron grip.

Without a word, he cut a small piece of chicken with his fork, then plucked it off his plate and held it to Tristan's lips.

"I'm not hungry." Tristan grumped.

"Eat."

Ben thought Tristan might push him further, but he didn't. Instead, he turned and curled into Ben's embrace, shrinking down as small as he could. Ben held the bite of food to Tristan's lips and after a breath, Tristan gently took the bite of food, his pretty pink tongue cleaned Ben's fingertips.

"Talk to me," Ben said.

Tristan chewed slowly, purposely dragging the bite out as

long as he could. He swallowed, then closed his eyes and clung to Ben. "I miss him. Which is stupid because he lives here, but he spends all his time working and avoiding us." Tristan gripped a handful of Ben's shirt.

"You still have feelings for him?"

The breath Tristan drew in shook. "I shouldn't. I can't. He left me, Ben. He left me and it hurt and I shouldn't care that he'll be moving out as soon as he can, but it feels like he's leaving me all over again. And it doesn't make sense." Tristan sucked in a deep breath. He opened his eyes and looked up at Ben. "Are you mad? That I brought him here? That there's still something there inside me that can't let go of him?"

Ben stroked Tristan's cheek with the back of his knuckles. "I'm not mad, love. Never. We can't control how we feel, you and I both know this."

Tristan gave Ben a watery smile. "You know I love you, right? I'd be lost without you. I'll get over this. I will. I just..." Tristan's gaze darted away. "I didn't think I still cared this much."

"It's easy to care about someone like Alex." Ben felt Tristan go still in his embrace and he kept talking. "He's a good man, one who tries hard to be self sufficient and independent. He doesn't want to need us, but I think he needs more from us than a place to stay."

Tristan looked up at Ben. "You... care about him?" Tristan snorted. "Of course you do. You care about everything I care about."

"It's not that, Tris. When he first came here, yeah, I cared about his well being because, one, I'm not an asshole, and two, I do care about the people and the things you care about. But he's grown on me."

"You want to take care of him."

Ben hid a smile in Tristan's hair. "You know me too well." Ben plucked another piece of chicken off the plate and held it to Tristan's lips. Tristan took a small bite and Ben finished the rest.

"What do we do?" Tristan sighed. "I don't think he wants much to do with us."

"I think you're wrong. You haven't seen the way he looks at you." Ben ran his fingers through Tristan's hair. "It reminds me of the way I look at you."

Tristan shook his head. "That's not funny, Ben."

"I wasn't joking." Ben drew Tristan in for a slow and tender kiss. "My poor boy, you're absolutely shattered, aren't you?" Ben spoke the words against Tristan's trembling lips.

Ben grunted as he stood with Tristan in his arms. He grunted with the effort, but he strode down the hallway, determined not to put Tristan down unless it was in bed. He wasn't that old and out of shape, heaving boxed of books at the store kept him in reasonable shape.

"What are you doing?" Tristan clung to Ben and laughed.

"Taking care of you."

"You're always taking care of me." Tristan's lips grazed Ben's cheek.

Ben pushed their bedroom door open with his foot and when he lowered Tristan onto the bed, he lowered himself on top of him. "I enjoy taking care of you." Ben whispered in the crook of Tristan's neck. Ben settled his weight on top of Tristan and held him tight.

Tristan breathed deep and Ben felt some of the tension bleed out of him. Ben ran his mouth along the slope of Tristan's neck until he reached the sensitive spot under Tristan's ear. He scraped his teeth over Tristan's flesh and his reward was a sweet moan and a needy boy arching into him.

"Someone sounds ready." Tristan moaned again when Ben ground their cock together. "Is there something you need, baby?"

"I need this plug out of my ass," Tristan's words warbled, and he clung to Ben. "Don't make me wait, please. Not tonight."

"Hush now," Ben cooed softly in Tristan's ear. "I've got you."

Ben moved and eased Tristan over onto his stomach. He

tugged at the loose pants Tristan wore and pulled them down Tristan's legs. He shoved them off Tristan's feet and Tristan kicked, pushing the garment onto the floor.

Ben climbed out of bed and ditched his clothes in a heap on the floor with Tristan's. He climbed back in bed slowly, taking the time to kiss his way up the back of Tristan's legs.

Ben pushed Tristan's legs apart and smoothed his hands up the insides of his thighs. Tristan's muscles twitched and trembled when Ben laved his tongue up the back of Tristan's balls. Tristan buried his moans into the mattress. Ben could almost see it in his mind, the way Tristan and Alex might look together. The way Tristan was shorter than either of them, and would fit perfectly between them, like a bridge, connecting them.

But Ben could also imagine Alex under him, pinned and desperate to get away. He wouldn't want to take what Ben wanted to give, because Alex didn't seem to believe he was worth much. Having him here in bed with Tristan by their side, Ben wanted to ravish them both. It didn't matter to Ben that Tristan and Alex had a history together. It might not make sense to anyone else, but that was the reason Ben wanted him.

Ben pulled Tristan's cheeks apart and looked at the base of the plug. He pressed on it and Tristan jumped and squeaked.

"That's... fuck, I'm close." Tristan panted.

Ben pulled at the base of the plug, not removing it, but easing it back before pushing it forward again. Tristan humped the mattress and Ben gave him a smack on the ass. "Stay still."

"Ben," Tristan whined and his muscles tensed with the effort it took him to stop moving.

"Mmm. Good boy."

"Ben, please." The words came out tangled in breathless laughter. "I'm going to come all over the bed."

Having a shred of mercy, Ben stopped toying with the plug and dragged it out of Tristan's ass. It popped free and Tristan's body sagged, his hole gaped before the ring of muscle tightened.

Ben pressed his finger inside, sinking slowly up to the knuckle. Tristan groaned long and low and stretched, his body gripping Ben's finger as if trying to urge more of Ben inside.

Ben removed his finger and moved up the bed. Tristan's hole waited for him, loose and lubed. Ben blanketed Tristan's body with his and lined his cock up. Ben wrapped his hand over Tristan's mouth and slid inside. Tristan's eyes screwed shut and puffs of air ghosted out over Ben's fingers.

Ben closed his eyes. If he could, he would etch Tristan's name into his bones. He was the most important thing in Ben's life, and sometimes he felt a bit like Icarus must have when he flew too close to the sun. His love for Tristan burned hot and bright. Tristan was his sun, the center of his universe. Ben had been pulled into Tristan's orbit and his life was infinitely better because of it.

And now, the possibility of someone else in the universe who knew what it was like to love Tristan down to their bones, who knew what they'd had, who might understand some of what Ben felt… it scared him. The idea of it was too much, too good to be true almost, that they could've found someone who might fit with them, not between them like an obstacle, but next to them to make a circle. And as exciting as the possibility was, it terrified Ben to want it.

Tristan arched underneath him, urging him to move. Ben smiled against Tristan's shoulder. "Impatient."

Tristan's laughter rumbled, and he mumbled something into the palm of Ben's hand. Ben ignored him and clamped tighter, sinking deeper with a sharp thrust of his hips.

A moan that sounded like a declaration of love spurred Ben to move faster. He pistoned his hips, drilling into Tristan over and over, chasing a closeness he couldn't quite reach.

Ben pulled out and grabbed Tristan, flipping him over. He spread Tristan's legs wide, making room for himself between them as he crashed their mouths together. He cradled Tristan's face in his hands and licked his way inside Tristan's mouth. Desperation burned under his skin and he ground against Tristan. He didn't want to stop kissing Tristan to get back inside him, but he made himself sit up and line his cock up with Tristan's hole again.

He watched bliss overtake Tristan's expression when he pressed back inside, back where he belonged. Ben wrapped a hand around Tristan's cock and stroked it with a lazy rhythm that matched the one he fucked Tristan with.

Tristan reached for Ben, pulling him down with a gentle tug of his fingers. Ben was lost to this man and his gentle kisses and quiet whimpers. With all the breadth and depth of his heart, Ben loved him and he did the best he could to pour every iota of that unquantifiable affection into the way he kissed and fucked and loved Tristan.

And Tristan loved him right back with tender kisses that grew desperate and moans that were as constant and needy. Ben held on and waited for Tristan to come first. He waited until Tristan shook and whined and wrapped his legs around Ben. He dug his heels into Ben's ass and urged him to go harder and deeper. And Tristan's moans spilled into Ben's mouth the way his cum spilled onto Ben's hand.

Ben pulled out of the kiss and buried his face in the curve of Tristan's neck as Tristan's fingers dug into Ben's hair and pressed into his scalp before they roamed down his neck and across his shoulders. And then Ben was coming too, with shudders and heaving breaths and emotion thick enough to choke on.

But he slowed his rhythm and eventually went still, still buried inside his love, still half hard, and he caught his breath. And he didn't choke. He lifted himself and propped himself up on an elbow. He cupped Tristan's face in his hand.

"I want to give you everything." Ben confessed. It wasn't a secret, but Tristan needed to hear it as much as Ben needed to say it.

Tristan's eyes softened in understanding. He leaned into Ben's touch. "You can't give me him."

Ben leaned down and brushed his lips against Tristan's. "I can give you the chance."

Tristan caught Ben in another kiss and when he pulled away, he looked up at Ben with glassy eyes. "Us the chance."

Ben tangled their fingers together. "Us."

14

TRISTAN

Ben pulled him close and kissed him before he left for the bookstore. Alex was still sleeping, probably because he'd been up half the night working. Tristan hated the hours he kept trying to get himself back onto his feet. But there was little he could do about it. Yet.

"Talk to him." Ben ghosted another kiss against Tristan's mouth.

"I will." Tristan bit his lip and Ben frowned at him. "I will. I promise."

"Good, because you're driving yourself into the ground worrying and wondering."

Tristan sighed and let his forehead rest on Ben's shoulder. "I know. But..."

"No what ifs. We've been over this. No more guessing. You need to talk to him."

"And you really think it's better if you're not here?"

After a pause, Ben said. "I don't have the history with him you do. I don't want him to feel ganged up on." He sounded unsure, something Tristan was used to seeing from Ben. His husband was always sure of everything.

Tristan pulled Ben close and pressed his lips to Ben's cheek. "I'll talk to him today, I promise." Come hell or high water, Tristan was going to make himself talk to Alex.

Ben exhaled, maybe with relief. Ben, for as in control of things as he was sometimes, had trouble dealing with negative emotions like fear. Tristan would have to be brave for both of them.

"Go," Tristan said, giving Ben a last kiss. "I'll text you."

Ben took a breath and nodded. "No matter what happens today, it's okay. We're okay."

Tristan nodded and flashed Ben what he had hoped would be a dazzling smile. "Love you."

"Love you, too." Ben stole another kiss and left, taking a portion of the air in the room with him.

Tristan didn't want to wake Alex up, but it made him antsy to have him close, but to feel that divide between them. He wanted to crawl into bed with him and wrap himself around him and remember what it felt like to be surrounded by his heat and his scent.

Today felt like it could be the ending of something, or the beginning, it could go either way. He raked his hand through his hair, noting to himself briefly that he needed a trim. Maybe today was both. Beginnings and endings didn't exist independently.

Tristan unloaded the dishwasher and tidied the kitchen. He busied himself in the living room, folding blankets and watching their television while dusting. Mostly, he was watching the clock, waiting for Alex.

He chuckled darkly and dropped into the recliner and buried his face in his hands. He'd promised himself, after Alex left, that he wouldn't wait for him. It was one promise he'd never been able to keep. He'd waited. He'd hoped Alex would come back to him, that they could forget he left and go back to what they had. But Alex had wanted things that weren't important to Tristan, and he'd wanted him to give up being close to his family, which was something Tristan couldn't give up.

He asked himself if he was insane for wanting Alex back now, after all these years. Maybe he was, but he didn't care. He looked at Alex and all he saw was someone he couldn't let go of. Someone who'd made him deliriously happy once. Someone who grew with him and laughed with him.

"Hey."

Tristan wrenched his head up and stared at Alex. He was sleep rumpled and gorgeous. He rubbed at his eye and glanced at the kitchen.

"Is there coffee?" Alex asked.

"Yeah." Tristan managed to say, though he felt tongue tied.

"You okay?" Alex squinted at him and dropped his hand to his side.

"Yeah. I'm fine."

Tristan didn't want to spring it on him before he'd had a cup of coffee, but the wait was killing him. He wanted Alex to be his again so much he could almost taste it. He'd waited this long, he could wait twenty more minutes.

Alex came out to the living room and sat on the couch opposite Tristan. He held the cup of dark brew in his hand and stared into it. Eventually, he lifted the cup and took a sip.

"You have that, we-need-to-talk, face on."

Tristan laughed. "Shut up."

Alex glanced at him and gave him a half-smile. "But I think I know what you're going to say."

Tristan blinked at Alex. Was he that obvious? He'd thought he'd held his cards close to his chest, but Alex knew him, so maybe he'd seen through him after all.

"I almost have enough to move out." Alex said. "I've been looking at apartments, and it won't be fancy, but I can manage. You and Ben have been amazing. I don't blame you for wanting your space back."

Tristan stared at Alex. He opened his mouth. Then closed it again. For a minute, he didn't know what to say. He buried his face in his hands and ran them through his hair, roughly tugging at the strands. He sucked in a deep breath, and then another.

"Do you.. do you want to leave?"

"We both know I've overstayed my welcome." Alex didn't sound dejected or upset, simply... depressingly accepting.

Tristan wanted to go to him, but he couldn't move. Fear and anxiety and all the things he had yet to say kept him pinned in place. "Alex. I don't... we don't want you to go."

Tristan's chest squeezed, and he felt like he was fighting for breath. All those years ago, Alex had left. Their conversation turned into a bitter fight, and it ended in tears and the ache of those moments still lived in Tristan and he felt them again keenly while staring across the room at Alex, who thought Tristan wanted him gone.

"You don't have to look after me anymore, Tristan. I can look out for myself." Alex straightened, suddenly defensive.

Nothing was going right. Alex wasn't supposed to be trying to leave him again. Tristan shouldn't be choking on his emotions. They were supposed to be talking, and maybe sorting things out, maybe coming together, or figuring out where they go from here.

"Alex. We don't want you to go, because we want you to stay." Tristan wet his lips and took a deep breath. "We want you to stay because, well... we like you." Tristan felt like a middle-schooler. He had half a mind to write a note on a piece of paper, asking Alex to be their boyfriend, yes or no. It would be easier than this torturous baring of soul. "We like you. We want... we want you around. We... I still have feelings for you. And Ben. Ben knows. And he likes you, too."

Alex stared at him with wide eyes, and he set his coffee down with a shaky hand.

"You can't be telling me this." Alex stood and the weight of unspoken words lifted, allowing Tristan to shoot to his feet and stop Alex's retreat. "Ben's not here. He's your husband. You love him. You don't love me. Please, he's good, you... you can't."

Tristan stepped in front of Alex and grabbed his biceps. "Alex, listen to me. Ben knows. He knows how I feel. He knows I'm talking to you today, and he knows how he feels about you, and he's as sure of this as I am. We want you to stay because we want you, Alex."

Alex shook his head. "No."

"Don't say no." Tristan pleaded.

"Ben's not here."

"He didn't want you to feel outnumbered. That's all." Or maybe Ben feared rejection as much as Tristan did. Maybe more so. Tristan should have made Ben stay for this, but Ben's leaving made sense at the time.

"You're married, Tristan." Alex's eyes shone. "You always wanted to be married. I won't be the reason you lose that. Ben and you, you're good together."

"We are. And so were we." Tristan slid his hands up Alex's arms and held his head in his hands. He needed Alex to hear him. "We can all be happy together. It's what Ben and I want.... if you want it, too."

For every second Alex didn't speak, Tristan's tenuous grasp on his emotions slipped. They were on a precipice and Tristan teetered on the edge between falling in love or falling apart. It felt like once again, the rest of his life depended on what Alex would say, and he was as afraid now as he'd been the first time he'd begged Alex to stay.

Alex shook his head and all the air left Tristan as if someone had kicked in the chest. This was it. He'd lost. He sucked in a deep breath and tried to be brave. Alex spoke before he could open his mouth.

"I need to talk to Ben. I can't... I can't say or do anything until

I talk to both of you. I can't think or talk or decide anything until I hear from him."

Tristan exhaled and hope coiled in his gut. "It's not a no?"

Alex looked pained and torn. Fuck. Ben really should have been here for this.

"Let's go talk to Ben." Tristan said, releasing Alex before he did something stupid like kiss him. He hoped in the time it took them to get dressed and get to the store that Alex wouldn't talk himself out of anything. "Get dressed. I'll drive us."

Alex turned away and Tristan spoke. "Don't... don't decide yet, okay. Please?"

Alex nodded and slipped into his room. The quiet clicking of the door shutting reverberated through Tristan like the impact of an explosion. He took a deep breath, then pulled his phone out of his pocket and texted Ben, warning him of their impending arrival and Alex's hesitation.

His hands shook when the phone ring and he fumbled as he answered, nearly dropping the phone.

"Ben?"

"Are you okay? Maggie should be here by the time you get here, unless you want to wait and I can come to you."

"We can't wait. Ben," Tristan glanced at the closed bedroom door and lowered his voice. "What if he says no?" What if he left? What if he walked away and Tristan never saw him again? He'd survived it once, and he knew he could again, but Tristan knew he didn't want just anyone to be with him and Ben. He wanted Alex.

"Deep breath, love. No matter what happens, no matter what he says, we'll deal with it together."

The bedroom door opened and Alex stepped out in a pair of jeans and a dark blue Henley Tristan had ordered because he knew it would look amazing on Alex.

"We'll be there soon," Tristan promised.

"Put Alex on for a second."

Tristan pulled the phone away from his ear and held it out toward Alex. "Ben wants to speak to you."

Alex took the phone hesitantly and cleared his throat before answering. "Hello?"

Tristan watched, and he strained to listen, but he couldn't hear what Ben was saying.

"Okay." Alex paused. "Yeah, okay, bye." Alex handed the phone back and Tristan pressed it to his ear.

"See you soon. Love you."

"Love you." Tristan stared at Alex when he said the words, maybe meaning them for Alex, too. The call ended and Tristan shoved his phone back in his pocket. Though he was dying to ask what Ben had said, he refrained. If Ben had wanted him to know, he'd have told him, or maybe Alex would offer the information willingly.

"Ready?" Tristan asked.

Alex nodded, and he followed him out to the car. Tristan didn't know what to say. He'd spilled his guts to Alex already, and now they couldn't do anything else, couldn't say anything else, either apparently, until they were with Ben.

The drive to the bookstore was the longest ten minutes of his life.

15

ALEX

This whole thing was madness. Alex had woken up and stepped into an alternate reality, one where Tristan and Ben had clearly lost their fucking minds. How was any of this real?

They parked in front of the bookstore, and Tristan killed the engine. He looked over at Alex, then reached across the car and took his hand. Alex looked down where their hands joined and fought against the way his body wanted to shake.

"This can't be real." Alex said, still staring at their joined hands.

"Come on, let's talk to Ben." Tristan reached for his door.

"You're sure about this? Alex tightened his grip on Tristan's hand. Though he'd been the one to throw him into this emotional storm, he was also Alex's lifeline. Did he like Ben and Tristan? Yes. Did he want to hear them out? Also yes. But was he absolutely shit-scared. No, because scared couldn't accurately describe the feeling of icy terror that ran up his spine.

What if he said yes? What if he said no? Why him? Why now?

"Come on," Tristan urged. "Ben's waiting on us."

Alex unbuckled his seat belt and climbed out of the car. He

mourned the loss of Tristan's hand in his, but didn't retake it. He needed space to think, something he couldn't do with Tristan touching him.

It was an innocent thing, but Alex hadn't had someone touch him in an eternity, and now Tristan had touched him a couple times that day, and he realized how much he missed it. Companionship. Touch. Being important to someone. It was almost enough to get him to agree to anything, even before speaking with Ben. But Alex wouldn't forgive himself if he came between the husbands.

The bookstore hadn't changed from the last time Alex was here. It was still quiet and clean with a few customer lingering in the stacks. Ben's gaze met his and Alex thought he looked... different. Nervous, maybe. Alex wiped a clammy hand on the side of his jeans. At least he wasn't the only one.

"Go on back, I'll be there in a minute." Ben said as the customers lined up at the register.

Alex followed Tristan to Ben's office and dropped on the couch that lined one wall because his legs had gone to jelly and he needed a minute to breathe.

Ben entered a few minutes later.

"I locked up." Ben went to his desk and leaned against it, then thought better of it and sat next to Alex on the couch. "Tristan talked to you."

Alex nodded.

"And he told you what we want?"

Alex nodded and licked his lips. Why were words so hard?

"But you don't believe him?" Ben studied Alex's face. He looked sad and concerned, yet somehow Alex saw a little hope in Ben's eyes.

"I want to believe, but I'm a mess, Ben. My life is currently shit, I'm working like a dog. I've saved every dime I've made and I still don't have enough." Alex raked his hands through his hair.

Then Ben reached over and took one of his hands. Tristan

squatted in front of Alex and cupped his cheek. God, how touch starved was he, Alex chided himself, as he leaned into Tristan's touch.

"We can go as slow as you want," Tristan assured him, stroking a thumb over Alex's cheek. "But we like you, Alex. We care about you. We want you to be a part of our lives, as more than a roommate."

"We do," Ben said.

"Why do you need me though? The two of you are the perfect couple. I don't want to get in the way."

"We don't think of you as someone who would get in the way. We see you as, not a missing piece, but an additional piece. Something to make a good thing even better." Tristan moved closer. He kneeled in front of Alex, his now glassy brown eyes shone up at Alex.

"How would it even work? And what if we broke up? I'd lose the only friends I have."

The admission left Alex feeling raw. He hadn't meant to say that, and he didn't know what prompted him to, but Ben put his hand on Alex's knee and Alex stopped breathing. Ben's calm demeanor comforted Alex. That alone made him want to say yes. But then there was the way Tristan looked at him. It wasn't the starry-eyed infatuation of youth. Alex didn't know what it was, but he liked it. He liked that these two men, with their perfect marriage and their happy life, wanted him to be part of it.

But he couldn't make himself say the words. He didn't deserve them, or any of this. He didn't deserve another chance with Tristan, not after he spectacularly fucked up the first time.

"I'd never abandon you, Alex." Tristan's voice was thick and Alex could hear the words Tristan didn't say.

He'd never abandon Alex the way Alex had abandoned him to chase a dream that came true, but then fell apart. How bitter he must look to people, how sad and lonely. Pathetic. To go from all his successes to living in his ex's spare room with nothing to his name but a meager bank account and a meager stack of clothing he didn't even buy himself.

"Look at me, Alex."

Alex obeyed Ben's gentle command.

"You're still our friend, you're still welcome to stay for however long you need to. No matter what your answer is, nothing will change. Even if we do this, and it doesn't work out, you won't lose us."

"I've always been there for you, Alex." Tristan took Alex's other hand in his and tangled their fingers together. "That won't ever change."

Undeserved, unwavering loyalty was who Tristan was. It was almost enough to make Alex say yes, but it also made him want to say no. Tristan had a devoted husband. Tristan might still have lingering feelings for Alex, but none of that mattered in the long run if Ben was only doing this to make Tristan happy.

Alex looked at Ben and tried to find any trace of insincerity. "And if we do this? How does it work?"

Ben leaned closer. His gaze flicked to Alex's mouth, then back to his eyes. Tristan squeezed Alex's hand as Ben leaned closer.

"We go slow, at whatever pace you're comfortable with. We talk a lot and take things as they come." Ben was almost kissing him. Tantalizingly close, yet Alex still thought of pulling back. Of saying no. Of telling them they were out of their minds, wasting their time on someone like him.

But then somehow, he leaned forward and his lips gently met Ben's. Tristan gasped. Alex trembled. And Ben, he cupped Alex's cheek and deepened the kiss. Their tongues hadn't gotten the memo yet, but Ben's lips moved against his, coaxing him, gently easing his fears and creating an entire set of new ones.

Alex pulled away reluctantly. Ben opened his eyes and smiled at Alex, a soft shy smile. His cheeks were rosy pink from blushing and Alex thought he looked cute as hell like that, kiss drunk and happy.

Tristan hovered close, and perhaps he should have been more scared of what it would mean to kiss his ex-boyfriend's husband, and then his ex-boyfriend, but he didn't have time to think before Tristan was gently prodding Alex to turn and look at him.

Morning light poured in the window behind Tristan, and it gave him a halo. Dust motes floated in the sun behind him, and it looked more like a dream than the unbelievable reality Alex had found himself in.

"Please say yes."

It didn't matter if Tristan meant say yes to the kiss, or to being with them, or to moving to Jupiter, whatever Tristan wanted in that moment, and any other, Alex wanted him to have it.

"Yeah, okay. Yes."

Tristan squeezed his eyes shut and his fingers trembled as they traced a path along Alex's neck to pull him that final few inches closer.

Alex thought he remembered what it was like to kiss Tristan, but maybe he'd forgotten. Or maybe he never knew, because Alex was sure he'd remember the way Tristan sighed, or the gentleness of his kisses, as if he feared chasing Alex away. For sure, he would've remembered the unrelenting breathlessness that pulled his chest tight.

Tristan pulled away and brushed his fingers over Alex's cheeks. With a little horror, and a lot of embarrassment, Alex realized he'd started crying. He brushed his tears away and sucked in a deep breath.

"Are you okay?" Ben rubbed his hand across Alex's shoulders.

"I'm… overwhelmed." Alex tried to laugh, but it came out weak and forced and fell a little flat. "I'm happy, and confused, and a lot of things I can't quite…" Alex waved a hand in the air. "I'm fine. I'm a bit of a mess."

Tristan laughed. "But now you're our mess, and we'll be as patient as you need us to be."

"So… now what?" The kisses, the conversations, they'd knocked his head for a loop.

"Now, you let our boyfriend take you out for breakfast." Ben stood and tugged Alex to his feet. "As much as I'd love to hang out in here all day and make out with the both of you, I have books to sell."

Alex remembered the nearly finished website. He'd been reluctant to show Ben and Tristan. What if they thought he was overstepping? But now, they were boyfriends. Alex felt his mouth tug upward into a rare smile.

"About that. When you get home, I have a surprise for you. It's not done yet, but I want you to see."

Ben looked at Tristan, who shrugged.

"Don't look at me, this is the first I've heard of it, too." Tristan hooked his arm around Alex's waist, then grabbed Ben's hand and pulled him close. Alex watched them kiss, a brief but affectionate brush of lips. Tristan pulled away and smiled at Ben.

"I think a special dinner tonight is in order," Ben said. Then he glanced at Alex before stealing a kiss.

"Can you grab that takeout baked macaroni Alex likes?"

"Consider it done, but I really must get back to work." Ben frowned. "I'll try to get out of here early tonight."

"There's no rush, Ben. I'm not going anywhere."

Tristan tugged Alex out of the office. "Except to breakfast with me. I know the perfect place."

Alex followed, and even with Tristan tangled around him, it was still like wandering in the Twilight Zone.

16

BEN

Something touched Ben's arm, making him jump.

"Ben."

He turned and gave Maggie a sheepish smile. "Hi. Sorry. What?"

She smiled at him. "Someone's off in La La Land. What's going on?"

Maggie was an employee, but after working together they'd become close friends. She was there for Ben when Eric left, and she danced with both him and Tristan at their wedding.

"You're going to think I've lost my mind."

"Try me. My baby sister is a drama major. I'm familiar with people doing outlandish things."

Ben took a breath and gave her a pointed look. "Do you remember when Tristan's ex had that apartment fire, and we took him in."

Maggie narrowed her eyes, immediately suspicious. "Yeah."

"We're sort of, well, Tristan and I… we're dating him now."

Maggie's face lit up, then came crashing down. "Wait. Wait, wait, wait. Tristan's ex-boyfriend is your new boyfriend? And you're okay with this?"

"It wasn't Tristan's idea, not completely." He wasn't sure he was ready to articulate why he felt attracted to Alex or why he sensed a connection to him. "Do you think we're insane?" Ben bit his lip.

"Benji, sweetheart, there's nothing wrong with wanting people, even your husband's ex. Is it what people normally do? No. But that doesn't make it wrong."

Maggie was wise beyond her years, not that he'd ever tell her that. Instead, he told her, "You know you're the only person who calls me Benji."

"I know," she grinned.

"Benji is a dog's name."

Her grin widened. "I know. I had a dog named Benji once. He was this cute little puff ball. Loyal to the end, sort of like you."

Ben frowned. "Do you mean loyal like me, or cute and fluffy like me?"

Maggie's eyes sparkled. "Yes."

"Thanks. I think."

"Seriously, what are you still doing here? Shouldn't you be hanging with your husband and your new boyfriend? You pay me to work, Ben, so go away and let me earn my money."

"Man, you're bossy."

Maggie straightened her spine and rolled her shoulders back, adding a full inch to her barely five foot tall stature. "I'm not bossy. I have leadership skills, Ben."

"Noted."

"Now get out of here. How can I flirt with all the cute customers if you're looming over me?"

"You're incorrigible."

"The word is amazing."

"An amazing pain in my ass."

Maggie beamed at him. "Thanks. I try."

"No Christmas bonus for you." Ben said as he walked back to his office to shut his computer down and grab his jacket.

Maggie's laughter followed him and when he came back out, she gave him a pointed look.

"You better not turn into Scrooge." Maggie warned playfully.

"I'm not afraid of ghosts."

"But are you afraid of teenage girls? I have sisters, Benji. All younger than me. And do you know how many friends those girls have? You'd never sleep again."

Ben's eyes widened. "You wouldn't."

"Hell hath no fury like an army of teenage girls. Think of them as pack animals, Ben. If you cut one of us, we all bleed."

"You are a frightening person, Maggie."

Maggie waggled her fingers at him. "Bye, Benji. Give Tristan a kiss for me."

Ben said goodbye and made a quiet mental note to pad her Christmas bonus this year, just in case.

Ben left the bookstore with a spring in his step and decided against telling Tristan he'd be home early. Instead, he walked down a block to the florist and picked two bouquets of flowers. It bugged Ben a little that he knew Tristan's favorite flowers were lilies, but he had no clue about Alex's. Tristan might know, but Ben wanted to learn these things himself.

He settled on a bouquet of sunflowers and colorful gerbera daisies for Alex. Something he hoped would remind Alex that life could be full of vibrance and beauty, if he let it.

Ben scoffed internally at his sentimentality and walked to his car. He made a last stop on the way home to grab something for dinner. He wanted to take his men out one day, but he didn't want Alex to feel rushed. But there was nothing rushed about a bouquet and a quiet night at home.

He didn't know what to expect when he got home. Most of the time, Alex stayed holed up in his room, tapping away on his computer. If Tristan was home, he'd be making dinner, or curled up on the couch with a book or a video game. Today, however, Ben opened the door to the sound of laughter. He smiled to himself and quietly shut the door. He toed his shoes off and poked his head around the corner.

Tristan and Alex were playing Mario Kart, again, and by the way Tristan leaned aggressively as he turned, he guessed Tristan was losing, again. Trying to keep his presence a secret, he sneaked into the kitchen and put the food on the counter where it would keep for a minute. He'd had the two bouquets of flowers pinned under his arm by the stems and he removed them carefully, checking for damage.

Ben returned to the living room to see Tristan and Alex, their mouths an inch apart. The tension between them made Ben's cock throb, and he stopped in his tracks. He wanted to see this, to see what it would look like to see them actually together. Alex's gaze was soft for Tristan and vulnerable. And Ben watched the moment slip away.

Alex spotted him and jumped back, putting distance between him and Tristan as if he'd caught them doing something wrong. Tristan, bless him, tugged Alex back and gave him a peck on the cheek.

"It's just Ben. He's home early. Probably got all sentimental and distracted." Tristan turned and looked at Ben, his face split into a goofy grin. "Flowers," Tristan cooed. He stood and tugged Alex to his feet. He towed him toward Ben, and Tristan took his bouquet of lilies from Ben with a kiss on the cheek. "You're the sweetest."

Ben cleared his throat to rid himself of a sudden knot of nerves. "I didn't know what your favorite flowers were."

Alex's cheeks turned crimson, and he tentatively took the flowers from Ben, their fingers brushing together. It made Ben's stomach flutter like a teenager with a crush.

"I've never got flowers before," he said, sounding almost confused.

Tristan, shining bright as always, said cheerfully, "There's a first time for everything. And now you can't say you've never received flowers before." He winked at Alex. "Let me put these in water."

Tristan took the flowers from Alex, who looked almost sad to part with them already, and practically skipped to the kitchen. "Ooh, you remembered dinner, too." Tristan called out.

"Can you pop that in the oven while you're in there to keep it warm?"

"Consider it done, love."

Ben's gaze hadn't moved away from Alex, who continued to shift uncomfortably. Fuck, Ben felt the awkward vibe thicken as they both continued to say nothing. Thankfully, Tristan returned, and he slid his arms around Ben from behind.

"Now that Ben is home, can we please see the surprise?" Tristan asked Alex.

Alex looked shy, but a little happy, and he braved a smile. "He's been bugging me non-stop for a hint. I forgot how annoying he could be." Alex grinned and set off down the hallway.

"You mean persistent," Tristan huffed.

"I said what I said." Alex disappeared into his room and returned a moment later with the laptop. He set it on the table, facing away from Ben and Tristan, and turned it on. "It's still in the rough stages, I need to make some cleaner graphics and I thought I could take some better pictures for it... and I'm not sure I overstepped, but I saw an opportunity and I went for it." Alex tapped away at the keys, then turned the computer to face Ben and Tristan.

"It's my store." Ben squinted at the screen. Fuck, he probably needed to get his eyes checked, and moved closer. "What is all this? I mean, it looks amazing, but I'm confused."

Alex moved closer. Hunched over, he tracked his finger across the mouse pad and clicked through a brand new website for Ben's bookstore.

"After I went to your store, I checked on its online presence and I didn't see much besides an announcement about the grand re-opening. And you have no presence on social media, so I thought I could get that going for you and create you a fancy new website. Then, when I was building it, I thought maybe if you had a system, you could fulfill online orders and in-person sales."

Ben gawked at the computer screen. Alex had done most of the work already, all he had to do was input the bookstore's current inventory and Ben could be up and running in no time.

"This is amazing." Ben pulled out a chair and sat down. He clicked through the website. "You have an option for curbside pickup. I never thought of that."

"It saves people time, and with flu season coming up, it could bring in additional business from people who are immunr-compromised, or who have mobility issues."

Ben turned to face Alex, and Alex went bright-red and rubbed at the back of his neck. "I know, I probably over thought everything. I went overboard and overstepped."

Ben stood up and put his hands on Alex's cheeks and he pulled him into a kiss. He felt Alex's shock, then his surrender as his lips softened under Ben's assault. Alex kissed him back, albeit hesitantly, and his hands trembled as they settled against Ben's waist.

Because he wanted to deepen the kiss, to push Alex against the wall and rut against him like a teenager, Ben forced himself to pull away. Their foreheads rested against each other and Ben let his eyes stay shut.

"Thank you," Ben whispered.

"It's not a big deal. I worked on it around my freelance stuff."

"I meant the kiss, but thank you for the website, and the kick in the pants to modernize my business and join social media. Though I have don't know how to keep up with all that."

Alex laughed. "You have a twenty-something working for you. I bet she'd be great at it."

"I'll make her earn that Christmas bonus this year." Ben knew

Maggie would be brilliant as the designated social media guru. "But you'll have to show me how this whole order system works."

"It'll be my pleasure."

Tristan came up beside them and slid an arm around each of them. "Is there room for one more?" He brushed a kiss against the corner of Alex's mouth.

"That depends," Ben said, arching an eyebrow.

"On what?" Tristan narrowed his eyes.

"On whether or not you let me use Wario."

Tristan rolled his eyes. "Fine, but I call Yoshi." Tristan glanced back and forth between Ben and Alex. "I can't believe the two of you think you can take me."

"Because we can." Alex scoffed and tugged Tristan toward the living room. Ben took another look at the computer screen and his heart melted a little. The more he got to know Alex, the more he liked him. Ben wasn't sure like, was a good enough word for the way he felt about Alex.

Tristan called to Ben to join them and saved him from the temptation to dissect that train of thought any further.

17

TRISTAN

Dinner had been sweet, if not a little awkward, with Tristan and Ben both wanting to shower Alex with affection, and not being able to go all in the way they wanted because they didn't want to scare him off or overwhelm him. And Alex, who took it like an only slightly embarrassed champ.

They decided on a movie, and the three of them curled up on the couch together. Alex on one end, Ben on the other, and Tristan stretched out in between them with his head on Ben's lap and his feet on Alex's.

Halfway through the movie, Ben nudged Tristan.

"He's sleeping."

Tristan lifted his head and peered down at Alex. His hand rest on Tristan's ankle, and the other propped his head up on the arm of the couch. It wasn't that late yet; still Tristan knew Alex had been burning the candle at both ends.

"Good." Tristan whispered and settled back into Ben's embrace. "He never sleeps. I swear he thinks he can survive off grit and determination. Maybe now that he has us, we can get him to slow down a little. I know he's eager to get back on his feet, and he's struggling, but he's going to make himself sick if he keeps going like this."

The movie played on in the background, explosions and gunfire filled the living room with sound and flashing lights, and still Alex slept.

"Looked like you two were about to kiss when I walked in." Ben stroked his fingers through Tristan's hair. It felt so good, Tristan wanted to purr like a spoiled cat.

"Mmhm. I think you coming home spooked him."

"We'll have to talk about rules and boundaries. I want him to know you two weren't doing anything wrong. I want the two of you to feel free to get closer, even if I'm not there."

Tristan rolled onto his back and looked up at Ben. "The same goes for you, Ben. I have a history with Alex to build on, but you and him are brand new to each other. I want you two to explore whatever's brewing between you."

Ben blushed and bit his lip. Fucking adorable, Tristan thought. "I know you like him," Tristan continued. "I like that you like him. And watching you kiss was fucking hot."

"Yeah?"

"Hell yeah. I don't mind taking things at Alex's speed."

"Delayed gratification."

"Oh yeah. So good." Tristan reached down and adjusted himself through his sweats. "I can't wait."

"Can't wait for what?" Alex said. He straightened up and rolled his neck, groaning in discomfort. "Oh, hell, that sucked."

"Can't wait for you to take your shirt off and sit on the floor and I'll rub that stiff neck of yours." Tristan sat up and squished himself against Ben's side. He spread his legs and made room for Alex to sit between them. "Come on, sit."

"I should probably get some work done," Alex hedged.

"Nope." Tristan stared him down and pointed to the spot on the floor between his feet. "Did you forget how persistent I can be? You've worked your ass off lately and you need a break. And I need to enjoy my new boyfriend. So sit."

"I must have wiped bossy Tristan from my memory." Alex grumbled, but peeled his shirt off and plopped himself somewhat gracelessly between Tristan's knees.

Tristan put his hands on Alex's shoulders and started off slow, with gentle pressure applied by his thumbs up the base of Alex's neck. Alex went limp almost instantly. His shoulders dropped, and he let his neck relax under Tristan's expert touch.

"Holy shit, you're still incredible at that."

Tristan let his chest puff up. "I've been practicing."

Alex made an incoherent sound of agreement as Tristan continued. While Alex was cooperative, it tempted Tristan to confront him about how much time he'd been working every day. But more than confronting him about his ridiculous hours, Tristan wanted to enjoy this peace between them.

They'd been together a few short hours and Tristan realized he was reining himself in with Alex. Tristan didn't want to lose Alex to old behaviors. He didn't want to lose him because he was too bossy, too demanding. But he also didn't want to lose Alex to his work again.

It had killed Tristan when Alex moved away. It killed him that Alex would leave, and it destroyed him when he couldn't make himself go. He knew love wasn't enough, even then, when it felt like the only thing. Tristan knew he didn't want to leave his family. Visiting a few times a year, maybe, wasn't what Tristan wanted. His parents had supported his decision, but sometimes he'd wondered if they'd quietly thought him to be a fool.

Then Tristan fell in love with Ben, then Eric. And after Eric, there was still Ben. The man who Tristan needed like he needed air. Ben was his proof that not everybody leaves. Ben stayed with him through it all. Including Tristan's confession that he'd always sort of wanted a relationship between more than two people. Ben had been his rock through the collapse of their relationship with

Eric. And even before Alex came back, Ben had known all about their history. He'd know that Tristan had feelings for Alex that would never go away. And he'd embraced all these experiences.

"You okay, babe?" Ben asked out of the blue.

Tristan faced him. "Fine, why?"

"You look upset."

Alex turned to face him. It was like being put on the spot. Tristan wasn't sure that he should say anything when he himself wasn't sure how he felt, but if this was to work, Tristan would have to get used to being unsure and communicating, anyway. What happened was in the past, and it didn't have to color their future together.

"I'm fine. I got stuck in the past for a second." Tristan gave Alex what he hoped was a reassuring smile. "I'm glad you're here with us, Alex. No matter what we had to go through to get here."

"Me too." Alex cleared his throat. "I have a lot of regrets about what happened between us, Tristan." His gaze shifted back and forth between Tristan and Ben. "But you're both making it hard to hang onto those feelings."

The words Alex spoke made Tristan's unease vanish like magic. Maybe it was foolish to go all in on someone who'd hurt him before, but it was too late for second guesses. Too late for take-backs because Tristan had already leaped off the edge and this time... he'd dragged Ben with him.

It had to work out.

Alex covered his mouth and yawned, wide and long. Tristan couldn't be the only one who noticed the bruise-dark bags under his eyes.

"You need more sleep." Tristan cupped Alex's chin in his hand and leaned down for a kiss.

"I have work to do." Alex tried protesting, but Tristan shook his head.

"Tonight you can sleep. The work will still be there in the morning."

"I'd listen to him, Alex." Ben offered gently. "He's worried about you. We're both worried about you. You've been working yourself to the bone. Take the night off."

Alex set his jaw, and it looked as though he were going to argue, but in the next moment he was yawning again. Tristan let his fingers slide through the short hairs at the back of Alex's neck. More than anything, he wanted to bring Alex to bed with him and bury him in between himself and Ben. Tristan ached to keep Alex close now that he had him.

Going slow was good, he kept telling himself. It was the opposite of the speed he wanted to do things, and he had to fight himself to not drop to the floor, crawl into Alex's lap and kiss him until they were dizzy and spent.

"I think I will turn in," Alex admitted defeat after another jaw-cracking yawn.

Tristan stole a kiss. "Sleep well." He bit back the invitation to join him and Ben. It would be easy to fall into that level of domesticity and intimacy.

"Thanks. You too." Alex flicked a tentative gaze toward Ben, but got to his feet and turned to walk away.

Ben caught Alex's fingers and tugged him back. He stood and brushed a kiss against the corner of Alex's mouth. "Good night, Alex. And for the record, you can kiss me whenever you want to."

Alex blushed and nodded before turning and retreating down the hallway. After a quick stop in the bathroom, Alex disappeared into his room and Tristan hoped he'd get a good sleep for a change. He felt almost tempted to hide the laptop to prevent Alex from getting up and working in the middle of the night, but Alex was an adult, and Tristan had to trust that he could look after himself.

"You did good today, love." Ben's arm wrapped around Tristan's shoulders and he drew him close.

Tristan melted into Ben's side and closed his eyes. "At what?"

"At not rushing Alex. I know you're all in, babe, and I know you and the things you want with him. And I'm proud of you for not taking this at the speed of light."

"He needs time to adjust." Tristan begrudgingly admitted. "Even if I don't."

Ben kissed the side of Tristan's head.

"I'm afraid." Tristan admitted quietly. "I'm shit scared that I'm already too invested in this working out, and that it won't, and that we'll lose him. And this time it will be worse, because you'll get hurt, too. And it will be my fault."

"I know you're scared, Tristan, but it'll be okay, no matter what. Because you will always have me. And we can get through anything together. But don't let the possibility of bad things ruin your enjoyment of the here and now. Right now, our boyfriend is hopefully sleeping in his bedroom. He's safe, he's here, and he has us now to care for him and help him. We'll take things one step at a time and it will work out."

Tristan exhaled, and tension bled away. "You always know what to say. How do you do that?"

"I'm smart."

"And humble."

"Oh, definitely humble. I think it's one of my best qualities."

"Your best quality is your taste in men." Tristan turned and draped himself over Ben's lap. He wound his arms around Ben's neck.

"You flatter yourself." If Ben's smile hadn't betrayed him, the twinkle in his eyes would have.

"Someone has to."

"How's this for flattery?" Ben clutched the back of Tristan's neck and pulled him into a kiss. He slid his tongue into Tristan's mouth and owned him with unrelenting passion. Tristan was breathless when Ben pulled away. His cock had leaked a wet spot into the front of his joggers, and Tristan was thankful he hadn't come in his pants.

"That'll do, I guess." Tristan fought the urge to touch his dick. Partly because he didn't want Ben to see how hard he was, even if Ben probably knew. He was also still perilously close to coming.

"You're a menace." Ben narrowed his gaze and tweaked Tristan's nipple.

Tristan yelped softly and covered his nipple with a hand. "And you like it."

"I love it, and you."

"I love you, too." And him, Tristan thought.

18

ALEX

By the time Alex crawled out of bed the next morning he'd almost convinced himself it had all been a dream, but when he stood at the coffeepot and Tristan wrapped his arms around him and kissed the back of his neck, Alex's insides lit up. It hadn't been a dream. It was suddenly the most real thing in the world.

"How d'you sleep?" Tristan mumbled the question into Alex's shoulder and pressed in tighter against him.

"Like the dead," Alex admitted.

"Good. You needed it."

Alex rolled his eyes. "I also need to get to work. I have a couple deadlines looming." Once he got these last few jobs wrapped up and he got paid, he'd have enough saved to get back on his feet. Money would still be tight, but at least he wouldn't be living in his ex-boyfriend's house. Alex smiled when the heat of Tristan pressed against him reminded him that was no longer true. Tristan wasn't an ex anymore. But Alex still needed to move out. He had to prove to Tristan and Ben that he could look after himself. That he had something of value to bring to the relationship.

"What are you working on right now?" Tristan slid in beside Alex and grabbed his coffee. He smiled at Alex as he stole a sip. "Just so you know, that's still disgusting."

Alex wrapped his hand around the mug. "Then don't be a caffeine thief. Get your own. And I'm working on a couple website designs, some new branding and logos for a few people. I have a few quotes to deliver, and some payments to chase. And I want to get the rest of the website set up for the bookstore."

"It looks amazing." Tristan let Alex pull away and he busied himself pouring a coffee. "I can't draw a stick man, let alone design an entire website. It's impressive."

Alex shrugged and sipped at his coffee so he wouldn't have to respond. "I've saved enough to replace my laptop. I'll shop around this week so you guys can have your computer back."

"It's not a rush, Alex. I don't use the computer ever, and Ben has one at work he uses for all the bookstore stuff. Besides, the laptop doesn't have Candy Crush."

Alex knew Tristan meant well, but instead of feeling good that he had all the time in the world, Alex's stomach clenched at the thought that Tristan didn't think he could provide for himself at all anymore. That he might not have faith in Alex's capabilities stung, and he tried not to let it show.

Alex had to prove to Tristan that he could still stand on his own two feet. He'd start by getting himself a new computer. Then he'd find an apartment and move out. And this time, he'd have renter's insurance. He'd prove to Tristan he was still worth having around, still worth caring for. That he could pull his own weight.

"You're lucky I have to work today, or I'd be dragging you to the couch to kick your ass in Mario Kart."

"You're a bad influence."

"I'm a good influence. All work and no play makes Jack a dull boy."

"I'm not about to go all The Shining on you, if that's what you're worried about."

"Well, I wasn't worried about that until now. I'll have Ben hide the axe."

"Why am I hiding the axe?" Ben came around the corner, his hair damp and messy from the shower. Alex's heart gave a funny jolt at the sight of him. Boyfriends, he had two of them now and they were both gorgeous.

"Tristan thinks I'm going to pull a Shining."

Ben arched an eyebrow. "Are you?" His brow furrowed. "I don't think we have an axe."

"See, you're safe." Alex told Tristan, who couldn't hide his amusement.

"I think we have a chainsaw." Ben chimed in with a wicked grin.

Tristan gaped at him. "You're the worst husband ever," he huffed.

Ben shrugged and blew Tristan a kiss. "But you love me, anyway."

"God knows why, must be that thing you do with your tongue."

Through willpower alone, Alex managed not to choke on his coffee. What exactly was the thing Ben could do with his tongue? He wanted to ask, but it felt intrusive. Though he had heard them have sex countless times since he'd moved in.

And one day he'd get to experience that with them. Fuck. Now he was hard. Alex hoped they were so wrapped up in themselves they wouldn't notice the state he was in. That his erection wasn't entirely inappropriate anymore was of little comfort to Alex. He wanted that with them, that naked intimacy, but it was far too soon to think of falling into bed with them.

Okay, so he'd already thought about it, but acting wasn't thinking. And if they saw how hard he was, to the point of pain while leaking in his fucking sweats, they might think he was ready for more. He wanted to be. It would be so easy. All he'd have to do would be to pull Tristan close and grind against him, and he knew from there Tristan would take over. He could still read Alex like a book. Like yesterday, the idea of kissing Tristan had barely crossed his mind when Tristan leaned in.

And then Ben came home and Alex had felt guilty, as if Ben had caught him with his hand in the cookie jar.

Maybe Ben was a mind reader now, because he called Alex's name and snapped him out of his stupor.

"Yeah? Sorry. I was thinking. You were saying?" Alex had a feeling he'd lost a bit of the conversation.

"I have a friend who can take new photos of the bookstore. Was there anything you had in mind? A style you wanted?"

Alex chewed on his lower lip while he thought. "What you have isn't bad, they're a bit out of date, that's all. You've updated the interior and the layout a bit since that series was taken. Something bright and clean is what you want."

"Noted. And this online system. When do you think you can have it up and running?"

"As soon as I get the inventory cataloged into the system, which shouldn't take long. Then we can launch the site and the new online ordering system all at once."

"I'll get Maggie started on the social media end of things." Ben frowned and sipped at his coffee. "I never intended to inherit a bookstore, so I've been winging it for years. Maybe a plan would be good."

"I can help with that." Alex nodded.

"While the two of you hash out bookstore stuff, I need to shower or I'll be late." Tristan drank the rest of his coffee in a few long gulps and set the cup in the sink. He leaned over and kissed Ben, then Alex before disappearing down the hall.

Alex watched him go. A funny feeling fluttered inside him. Before he could think too much about it, Ben spoke.

"He's happy." Alex looked at Ben. "I'm happy," Ben said.

"Me too." It was hard to admit, because happiness didn't last, so noticing it or mentioning it felt a little like throwing a jinx out into the universe. A challenge to swoop in and fuck with Alex again. But he couldn't look Ben in the face and lie.

"Come to the bookstore with me today. We can get started on that system of yours, and you can give Maggie all the info she'll need and we can work out what I owe you."

Alex flinched. "No, Ben, this was a gift. I can't take money from you."

Ben's eyes turned stormy. "I don't expect you to work for free."

"It's called a gift for a reason, Ben." Alex wrapped his arms around himself. "I wasn't doing it to get money from you. You've given me so much, I wanted a way to show my appreciation. Please... let me do this for you."

Ben's nod came after a long hesitation. "Okay."

"If it will make you feel better, give Maggie a bonus for putting up with your archaic, unorganized, ass." Alex laughed.

"Archaic?" Ben put his hand over his heart. "You wound me."

"Says the guy whose store has almost zero online footprint."

"Ouch. Okay, point taken. Good thing I have you to look out for me now." Ben moved in closer. Alex imagined Ben pressing him against the counter and trapping him there.

Ben was sweeter than Alex could've imagined. He leaned in and brushed his lips against Alex's gently with a slight hesitation that made Alex lean in and kiss him back, harder and hungrier. Showing him it was okay, that Alex was ready for this, for more. For kissing and being close. He still wasn't sure of all the rules, but he'd follow Tristan and Ben's lead.

Ben stepped closer and wound his arms around Alex. Pulling him close, he deepened the kiss. For a moment, their tongues brushed together, dancing and caressing and Alex lost the ability to think or breathe.

Then the kiss ended, but Ben pressed his forehead against

Alex's. Alex let himself enjoy this fleeting moment of peace and happiness.

"I'm glad you're here." Ben kissed Alex's cheek and pulled away. He smiled at Alex. "I wanted you to know that."

Ben disappeared down the hallway, giving Alex some breathing room. Alex rinsed the cups and stacked them neatly in the dishwasher. He put his palms on the counter and exhaled. How was this his life now?

Sometimes he felt like he'd gone from one disaster to another. A failed career. A foreclosure. Two cross-country moves. A soul-splitting break up. An apartment fire. Could this really be the beginning of something better? It terrified Alex to think he could trust it. Every time he settled into his existence, life threw him a curveball and knocked him down. Were it not for Tristan and Ben, Alex wasn't sure he'd have been able to pick himself up this time.

And now it wasn't only his life that would fall apart if he fucked things up. Ben and Tristan's marriage could be on the line if shit went south. Alex exhaled, unsure of what to do, of how to move forward.

Tristan walked in, looking hot as sin in his EMT uniform. His hair was getting a little long and Alex wanted to brush the stray strands off his forehead.

"Have a good day, Tristan." Alex made the first move this time, compelled to grab whatever scrap of affection and happiness he could get before it faded away or disappeared. Because it would. It always did. But he could have this moment where he pressed his lips against Tristan's and wrapped his arms around Tristan's neck and kissed him before he left for work, as if it were something they always did. Or something they always would do. Something routine that might become mundane one day, if given a chance.

"Stay safe," he told Tristan as he pulled away.

Tristan dazzled him with a smile and stole another kiss. "You too. Look after my husband for me." Tristan winked and left, taking part of Alex's heart with him.

Happiness was fleeting and fragile, Alex knew it better than anyone. Delicate and delicious, Alex was afraid to feel this way, this light. Like things were possible. Good things. For a change, Alex didn't fear the sense of impending doom that would inevitably sweep in to press down on him and grind him into dust. However short-lived it might be, Alex was happy.

19

BEN

Alex stood at the counter with Maggie. They huddled over Maggie's phone, probably talking about the social media campaign they were launching along with the new website. Tomorrow was the grand unveiling of the new online ordering system and the curbside pickup. Ben was nervous about it, but Alex and Maggie had more faith and enthusiasm than they knew what to do with.

Ben's cell vibrated in his pocket and he answered with a smile after he saw Tristan's name flash up on the screen. He was at work, but if he had a spare moment, it wasn't unusual for him to call.

"Hey, babe. What's up?"

"Hey, so mom called. She's arranging this charity thing and some of her volunteers didn't show for the setup."

"Where is she?"

"She's at the hall down from the house. Do you know the place?"

"Yeah. What does she need?"

"Strong backs. She needs tables and chairs moved around and

set up. And Dad threw his back out last night, so he's out of commission."

"I'll bring Alex with me."

"She'll love that. You two are lifesavers."

Ben snorted. "Says the actual lifesaver."

"Takes one to know one."

Ben relished the warmth in Tristan's voice, the way he could say he loved Ben without saying it. The way he could make him feel things even when there was a distance between them and life going on around them. Tristan never let Ben forget how he felt about him.

"I love you," Ben needed to say it, in case he didn't have the same magical power Tristan possessed.

"I love you, too. Tell Mom we'll do lunch soon, okay? I have to go. Carter is giving me the stink-eye."

Ben laughed. Carter was Tristan's coworker, and he didn't have such a thing as a stink-eye. He was the most easy-going guy on the planet.

"I will. See you after work." The call ended and Ben made his way over to where Maggie and Alex still huddled as they chatted about marketing strategies. "We have marching orders," Ben said to Alex. "Tristan's mom needs a favor."

Alex straightened and nodded. "Sure. We were about done here anyway. Maggie knows what she's doing."

Maggie rolled her eyes. "Of course, I know what I'm doing."

Alex's face flushed at her words, and Ben slipped an arm around his waist to reassure him he had said nothing wrong. "Go easy on the fresh meat, Maggie, or I'll give him your Christmas bonus."

Maggie glared at Ben. "Hordes of teenage girls, Ben. Screaming and giggling."

"You play dirty." Ben said while tugging Alex away. "Come on, duty calls."

"Sure, sure, abandon your best employee during rush hour."

It was Ben's turn to roll his eyes. "You're my only employee, and there's two customers in here. If you can't handle that, you definitely aren't getting a bonus. Maybe I'll make you give me a bonus."

"You're a cruel, cruel man."

"I'm the best boss ever." Ben pulled Alex out of the store.

"What does Mom need help with?" Alex asked.

Ben nearly tripped over his feet to hear Alex refer to Bonnie as mom. "She's setting the hall up for some fundraiser event, but her volunteers bailed and Greg threw his back out last night. She needs some muscle."

"Did Tristan ever tell you about the goose shit?"

Ben unlocked the car and frowned at Alex. "No."

"God, it was terrible." They climbed into the car and buckled in before Alex continued the story. "She was setting up a fundraiser for the children's hospital. A huge outdoor barbeque. And she thought, since the forecast said the weather would be great, she'd have it at the lake. But a group of Canadian geese had migrated and taken up residence there."

Ben groaned. "No."

"Oh yes. Goose shit beach. It was everywhere. Greasy, black, and stinky. Tristan got this frantic call from Mom telling us to bring shovels and rakes. Worst day ever." Alex visibly shuddered in the passenger seat. "But she baked us lemon meringue pie as a reward for our hard work, so it was totally worth it. But I'm thankful that was the last time she tried to do an event by the water."

The question had weighed on Ben the last time they'd been around Tristan's family together. He'd rolled it around in his mind and decided there was no harm in asking.

"Is it weird, to call Bonnie mom? I mean, doesn't your mom mind?"

Alex snorted. "My mom? Nah. We don't get along well. Never

did. She's never been there for me. I haven't even talked to her since before I moved back here."

"Doesn't it make you... sad sometimes? To see how good Tristan's family is, how accepting and warm they are, and then think of your own shit-ass relatives and wonder why they can't be like that?"

Ben glanced at Alex and saw the way he chewed on his lower lip.

"Forget I asked. It's not important."

"No, I don't mind. See..." Alex paused and took a deep breath. He exhaled heavily before continuing. "Tristan has this great family. They're not perfect, but they give a shit about people. And at first it felt really fucked up, you know. You walk into this house and Tristan's mom is there shoving food at you, asking if you need anything. Making you comfortable and fussing over you. And his Dad is there, reading a fucking paper on his phone, quietly going along with all her many whims. And they love their kids. Even when the fuck up. And they have a way of making you feel like one of them."

Alex went quiet and Ben tried to digest everything Alex had said. It had been that way for Ben, too. The first time he'd met Tristan's parents, he'd been overwhelmed about how warm they were. Ben's family home was a house of eggshells and carefully drawn battle lines that no one dared cross. No one wanted to be the person to rock the boat. Least of all Ben. He hadn't known how liberated he'd feel by leaving until after he did.

"It's not weird for me to call her Mom, because that's how I see her. She's... she's been more of a mom to me than my own. And when I left, that was harder than I expected it to be. And I wanted to keep in touch because I missed them, but I couldn't because I didn't think they'd want to hear from me."

Ben reached over and put his hand on Alex's thigh. Alex covered it with his own.

"But she did."

Alex laughed. "When you two brought me over last time, she gave me a dressing down for not keeping in touch. She said she forgave me, and she understood, but that I wasn't to do it again." Alex wrapped his fingers up with Ben's. "What about you?"

"What about me?"

"You call them by their names. I know she's probably argued with you about calling her mom."

Ben smiled. "A few times. It felt, not like a betrayal to my mom, but like... Tristan's mom deserves better than that from me. To be that, you know. My mom held more firmly to her convictions than to her kids. But the rest of the family is the same. She's always been desperate to fit, you know."

Ben flicked on his turn signal and pulled into the hall. Tristan's mom waited out front and her face lit up when she saw them pull in.

Ben pulled the car into a parking space and killed the engine.

Alex undid his seatbelt and reached for the door handle but stopped and looked at Ben. "I know you have your own feelings about things, Ben. But you deserve to have a mom as great as her."

Ben sat there for a second, recovering from the gut-punch Alex's words had delivered. He'd never once stopped to think about what he deserved. He hadn't had the greatest family, and they'd only grown further apart since the move. Ben didn't want to think that any of their thinly veiled hate might have gotten to him, but it was hard to say it hadn't. Faced with a woman so warm and loving as Bonnie, Ben could have embraced the fact that she took everyone under her wing. She had more than enough love to go around, but Ben had decided that she deserved better. Better than him.

Better than him.

Better than him.

The words got stuck on a loop in his head as he climbed out of the car. Alex was right. Ben deserved more. He deserved a family who loved him. Parents who accepted him, who loved him for who he was, not despite it. Parents like Tristan's, who'd been there for him in a million different ways, big and small, from the day they'd met him.

Ben found a smiling Bonnie talking animatedly with Alex. Already he was pushing his sleeves up, getting ready to be put to work. Ben, without thinking, came up beside Alex and slid his arm around Alex's waist.

"Where do you need us?" Ben asked. Alex stiffened beside him, and Ben gave him a reassuring squeeze.

"I was telling Alex that I need the decorations hung, then the tables and chairs set up. I have a group on the way this evening to dress the tables. But I can't handle all those chairs myself. My poor old back aches thinking about it." Bonnie's eyes shone with a thousand questions, but she didn't pry. Ben could tell she was pleased, though, from the way she kept trying to douse her smile.

Bonnie hadn't been at all surprised or put off when Ben and Tristan had been dating Eric, and when he broke up with them, she was just as sad to see him go as they had been. Her unwavering support now bolstered Ben's mood. Maybe he never realized how much her approval meant to him, but he felt it now, burning bright inside him, making him feel as though he glowed and everyone could see.

Alex was right. Ben deserved a family like this one. A family who gave a shit about him when his own hadn't.

Ben couldn't put his gratitude for either of them into words, so he nodded at Bonnie and cleared his throat. "We'll get started on those decorations. Tell us what you need and we'll get it done."

Bonnie sighed with relief. "I knew I could count on you boys." Bonnie led them into the hall and explained what decorations they had and where she wanted them hung. Then she handed Ben a diagram that showed the layout of the tables. "Will you two be fine here for a bit while I go back and check on Greg?"

"We'll be fine," Ben promised.

With a parting glance and a pat on the arm, Bonnie stepped away and Alex finally relaxed beside him.

"Did Tristan tell her about us?" Alex asked quietly, as if he were a secret that needed to be kept.

"Of course he did. He tells his mom everything."

"And she's okay with it?"

"Don't sound so surprised. You know Bonnie, she's the greatest. She knew we were with Eric, and she didn't really bat an eye at that either. She wants her kids to be happy."

Alex turned to him and looked at him with eyes full of softness. "Yeah, she does. All her kids," he nudged Ben to drive his point home.

"Yeah, yeah." Ben shoved a glimmer of shame away. Bonnie wouldn't hold it against him that he hadn't called her Mom or hadn't wanted her associated with a person in Ben's life who'd never deserved the title she'd been given. But she would mind that Ben had thought of himself as undeserving.

He might never really believe he deserved people as wonderful as Bonnie and Greg, and Tristan and Alex, but he wanted to try. He wanted to believe that he did, that he was worthy.

"You okay?" Alex stopped him during the afternoon and asked. He put his hand on Ben's arm to stop him from the task he'd been doing.

Ben stole a kiss, smiling at the redness that crept across Alex's cheeks. "I'm good. I promise."

20

TRISTAN

"What did you do to my husband?" Tristan leaned in and asked when Ben excused himself to use the restroom of the steakhouse they were currently dining in. He kept his voice low, almost a whisper.

"What do you mean?" Alex asked, looking a little alarmed.

"He's… I don't know. Different. Lighter. Happy."

Alex shrugged. "We talked about stuff. Nothing huge. I didn't even say much."

Tristan tangled his fingers together with Alex's. "Well, whatever you said, thank you."

Alex tried to hide his blush by sipping at his water.

"I don't think you give yourself enough credit, Alex." Tristan moved his foot so it pressed against Alex's under the table. They were miles away from the groping twenty-somethings they used to be, who would play footsies in public, along with other things. And though most of the thrill of that had faded away, Tristan couldn't help the shiver that rolled up his spine like lightning when Alex's blush deepened. Clearly, he wasn't the only one who remembered their youth.

Tristan slid the toe of his shoe up the outside of Alex's leg.

Alex narrowed his eyes, but his hand trembled as he lowered his water to the table. "Stop it," he hissed.

"Stop what?" Ben asked innocently as he took his chair.

"Nothing." Tristan answered.

At the same time Alex said, "He's playing footsies with me."

Ben looked at Tristan. "Really?" Before Tristan could feel a stab of guilt, Ben continued. "You started without me."

If they kept this up, Alex looked like he might spontaneously combust. Tristan held Alex's hand tighter, hoping to telegraph how happy he was to have Alex with them. God, he wanted Alex to be with them in all the ways. Tristan was greedy for him, for his presence and his touch. He felt starved for Alex, and now he was so close. Still, they hadn't made that final leap. Tristan wanted that more than anything. He wanted Alex in their bed, in their room, forever. It was childishly romantic and Tristan knew it, but something about Alex made him feel that way. Greedy and young and even a little reckless.

"I can't wait to get you home." Tristan brought Alex's hand to his mouth and brushed a kiss against his knuckles.

The waiter arrived then with their dinner and Alex pulled his hand away from Tristan's, blushing furiously.

"I don't think I've ever seen you blush this much," Tristan remarked as he picked up his fork and stabbed his steak.

"I've never been on a date with a married couple before." Alex glanced around as he spoke, like he was doing something bad and afraid of getting caught. "What if people notice?"

"Does that bother you?" Ben asked. Tristan admired his husband for his ability to stay calm and collected about everything. Tristan kept his emotions in check at work, but he couldn't seem to put that sort of emotional barrier up any other time. But Ben, he was strong and stoic and forthcoming.

Alex cut into his steak. "Not as much as it should?" He posed it as a question and looked to Ben for an answer.

"Should it bother you? We're all in agreement about what we

are to each other, no one is hiding anything. No one is being unfaithful to anyone. So," Ben paused. "Should it bother you? It doesn't bother us." Ben's voice dipped lower. "Quite the opposite actually."

Alex shoved a bite of food in his mouth, probably so he wouldn't have to respond to Ben's blatant insinuation. His voice oozed with sex and want. It made Tristan's dick hard seeing the way he wanted Alex.

But Alex was skittish, like a barn cat, like he didn't trust the kindness of the humans who wanted nothing more than to shower him with affection. Tristan wouldn't risk injury in a public place. His feelings were too close to the surface, too raw and real and ready to overflow.

But when they got home, and the door shut behind them, and the deadbolt clicked into place, Tristan slid out of his jacket and stepped toward Alex. He crowded him against the wall and looked him in the eyes.

"Tell me to stop," Tristan leaned so close the command was a whisper against the corner of Alex's mouth.

Alex clutched Tristan's hips and pulled him in, closing the gap and sealing their mouths together. Tristan thrust his fingers through Alex's hair and deepened the kiss with a swipe of his tongue.

Trembling legs slotted Alex against the wall and he prayed he had the strength to hold himself up. Kissing Alex the way he wanted to, letting his ferocious desperation take over, made his knees weak.

Alex pulled back and Tristan clung to him, willing him not to say no. Not to push Tristan away. He would stop. He would do whatever it took to make Alex comfortable, but the longer it took him to get there, the more Tristan feared it would never happen.

Logically, he knew sex wouldn't make things better. It wouldn't make him stay if he didn't want to. But it felt like a barrier between them. Like it was the one thing keeping them apart. He yearned to be Ben, Tristan, and Alex. Three people. One relationship. Not two people with a third.

His mind raced faster than his heart, and he sucked in a deep breath.

"Is that a no?" He asked, terrified of the answer.

"It's a, can we move to where the knob of the closet door isn't driving into my back?"

Tristan huffed out a soft, relieved laugh and toed out of his shoes and tugged Alex down the hall. "Bedroom?"

The yes was breathy and barely there, but Alex looked back and reached for Ben. A wordless need sparked through the air between his men and Tristan's tension eased. This was really going to happen.

Tristan tugged Alex into the bedroom and backed up until he could sit on the mattress. He held tight to Alex's hand and looked up at him. Alex tangled their fingers together and Tristan tugged him closer. He put his other hand on Alex's hip and brushed his thumb under Alex's shirt, skating it along the smooth skin at his waist.

"Nothing you're not ready for." Tristan promised him. Part of him wanted to wrap his arms around Alex's middle and stay there, holding him like that and pretend they could exist like that for an eternity. But more than that, he wanted to taste his skin, his lips, his sighs. He wanted all of Alex and Ben. Gentle, sweet, Ben, who came up behind Alex and slipped his arms around him.

Tristan watched Alex's eyes flutter shut.

"Let us take care of you, Alex." Ben whispered the words in the dim room and Tristan couldn't miss the way Alex shivered when Ben spoke. Tristan untangled their fingers, then popped the button on Alex's pants and barely stopped himself from tearing them off.

Instead, he slowly drew the zipper down, looking up at Alex's dark eyes the whole time. Alex swallowed roughly as he watched

Ben ease the folds of fabric aside and lean in, mouthing Alex's cock through his briefs.

Tristan shuddered when Alex sank his fingers into Tristan's hair, raking them gently over his scalp. He wanted to lean into the warmth of his hands like a touch starved cat. Instead, he tugged at the waistband of Alex's briefs and pulled them down far enough to release Alex gently from their confines.

Alex's cock jutted straight out from his body, thick and hot. The head glistened with precum. Tristan dug his fingers into Alex's sides, then leaned in and swiped the head of Alex's cock with his tongue.

Alex jerked in his grip, his hips thrusting forward. Ben's hands slid up Alex's torso, gently divesting him of his shirt. As badly as Tristan had wanted to get to this moment, he was happy to drag it out and make it last. He wanted to luxuriate in Alex's taste, slightly salty, not at all unpleasant. And his sounds, delicate and sweet, hesitant too, like he shared Tristan's fears. That made Tristan feel better, less alone, less afraid of everything falling apart. Because if he wasn't the only one afraid, he wouldn't be the only one trying to hold them all together.

Alex's cock bobbed in the air and brushed against Tristan's cheek. He parted his lips and took the head into his mouth, eliciting a groan from Alex. Tristan closed his eyes and let the world drop away. Nothing existed but the cock in his mouth and the men in front of him. Alex whimpered from time to time, as Tristan slowly took him deeper into his mouth, then pulled away, swirling his tongue and caressing Alex's thick, veiny cock.

Alex's fingers kept tugging on Tristan's hair, gentle pulls, like he wanted more, but couldn't ask. Couldn't make himself admit he wanted more. And maybe he liked things differently than he used to. But in case he didn't, Tristan chanced it. He shoved Alex's cock deeper, forcing the head down his throat where he swallowed around it.

"Fuck," Alex swore and curled around Tristan momentarily.

Tristan pulled back and let Alex's cock slip from his mouth. Tristan looked up at Alex and flicked the end of Alex's cock with his tongue, smiling at the way it made Alex flinch.

"Problem?" Tristan couldn't keep the smile from his face. He felt cheeky and warm all over and happier than he'd ever been.

"Yeah, you're wearing too many clothes." Alex plucked at the collar of Tristan's shirt. He looked over his shoulder at Ben. "You too," his voice was thick and husky and sexier than Tristan remembered it.

He wasted no time peeling his shirt off and tossing it aside. After that, he couldn't wait. His need had become a tangible thing inside him, stoking his desires until his entire body burned hot and he shook with want as he took Alex back into his mouth.

Alex's hips jerked and Tristan hummed, encouraging him to take what he wanted, enticing him to fall into the pleasure of Tristan's wet mouth around his cock. Tristan's hands explored Alex's body. He smoothed them upward, mapping the way his sides were soft, undefined, and perfect. His nipples were rock hard and Alex hissed when Tristan's fingers brushed against them.

Tristan slid his hands down Alex's back and clutched his ass. He pulled Alex into him. Alex's hands clutched at Tristan's skull.

"Tris, fuck, Tristan, slow down. Not yet. Can't come yet." Alex have begged, half babbled.

Tristan pulled away and looked up and saw Alex, with his head tilted to the side, allowing Ben access to nibble and suck at his neck. It was a fetish of Ben's, the slope of a neck, the little spot below the ear, the corner of the jaw. Alex looked well fucked already with his unruly hair, his wide eyes and his parted lips that gasped when Ben sucked at his earlobe.

Alex turned and pulled Ben into a kiss, not a shy thing like they'd shared previously. This one was all hunger and heavy breaths. Eager mouths and busy hands, stroking every expanse of bare flesh, pulling each other closer, kissing harder, deeper. Their hips rocked and Tristan watched them chase friction.

Tristan watched the kiss end. Alex looked into Ben's eyes for a moment, and it felt more voyeuristic to witness that tender moment than it had felt to watch them rut against each other. Then Alex turned and looked at Tristan. He bent down and captured Tristan's mouth with his, eagerly licking his way inside. He pulled back too soon and Tristan whimpered.

"Get on the bed, Tristan." Alex begged.

Tristan wasted no time obeying. He scrambled backward, marveling at the way Alex followed him, like a moth chasing a flame, and when Tristan finally collapsed with his head on the pillows, Alex was straddling him, fumbling with the button of Tristan's pants, kissing him hungrily.

The bed dipped again, this time with Ben's weight, and once Alex got Tristan's pants undone, Ben was there, urging Tristan to lift his hips and helping Alex disrobe Tristan.

This couldn't be real. It was too good. Too bright. Too much. Too everything. Tristan's thoughts raced through all the reasons this couldn't be happening. One man didn't deserve this much happiness. But then Alex moved lower and spread Tristan's legs apart, making room for himself to slot in between them. He kissed the inside of Tristan's thigh and Tristan wanted to watch, but then Ben was there too, next to him.

A finger dragged down his cheek, and he made Tristan turn his head. The kiss Ben gave him was pillowy soft, achingly sweet, and everything Tristan needed to feel in that tender, dream-like moment.

He wanted to ask Ben if this was really happening. It still felt too good to be true, but there was no lie in the kiss Ben gave him, or in the way Alex's breath puffed out against the inside of Tristan's thigh, then in the crease of his leg as Alex kissed his way around, teasing Tristan with gentle brushes of his lips. This was the most real, most true thing Tristan had ever felt, this bright, overflowing love he felt for both men.

If he weren't laying down, it would have brought him to his knees. It was too soon to tell Alex he loved him. Still loved him. Never stopped. Never wavered; always wondered. Too soon for any of that, because he still hadn't told Ben exactly how he felt, because he hadn't been sure of it himself. But now it was so fucking obvious Tristan wanted to shout it from the rooftops. He'd dreamed of this, of having Alex in his life again. In his bed, his arms, his heart. At the breakfast table and out for dinner. But the reality was so much better than the dream, Tristan thought, when Alex took Tristan's cock into his mouth and his gentle touch slid between Tristan's legs and cupped his balls.

Ben kissed Tristan as though he might die if he stopped, and Tristan hoped that one day, Ben might love Alex as much as he did.

21

ALEX

Dinner had been nothing but nervous energy. Shy glances passed between the three of them. He'd avoided thinking too much about this moment and what it would mean. What it would change. The only thing he wanted to think about was the rightness of it all as he moved down Tristan's body, lavishing attention to the man's smooth skin. He nuzzled in against Tristan's belly button before following the dark treasure trail lower.

Ben had helped strip Tristan, his own husband, so Alex could enjoy all of him. Alex knew he didn't deserve any of this. Nothing he'd done had led to him earning any of this. These men or their affection. Their help. They'd opened their home to him, their lives, everything.

Alex knew he wasn't good enough for them. He never was, and maybe he never would be. But in moments like this, with Tristan trembling beneath him, he almost thought he belonged. He wanted to. More than anything, he wished that this could be his place forever. He'd fallen for Tristan all over again. It wasn't hard, considering he'd never truly let go of his feelings. But Ben, he was a surprise.

Alex never considered himself to be a man who could want more than one person. It had always been Tristan for him. And now there was Ben, too. Their lives and hearts inexplicably tangled around his own.

Alex looked up and watched Ben and Tristan kiss. He didn't feel left out, couldn't, not with Tristan's hand playing with Alex's hair, urging him to do something with his mouth. Alex licked his way up Tristan's cock from root to tip before sliding it over his tongue and past his lips.

Tristan's hips bucked, and Alex's heart fluttered. He let his eyes close and he fell into the enjoyment of Tristan, of pleasuring him with his tongue and lips, with gentle sucks and deep slides down to the back of Alex's mouth.

"Alex."

Alex raised his gaze at the sound of his name. Tristan stared down at him with inky black eyes. He'd propped himself up on his elbows, but he reached for Alex at the same time as he said, "Come here."

When Alex had crawled close enough, Tristan fell back on the bed and cradled Alex's face in his hands, pulling him into a kiss so deep Alex risked losing himself forever in it.

Tristan wrapped a leg around Alex and pulled him close, angling their bodies together before he started rocking and undulating beneath him. The friction almost did Alex's head in. As it was, the world spun beneath him, or maybe it was Tristan's kiss that made him dizzy.

"I've dreamed of this," Tristan confessed in the dimly lit room, his husband kneeling by his side, another man, his ex, on top of him, naked and leaking. Alex sat up, struck by the words and the weight of truth behind them. Then, Ben leaned closer, and he pulled Alex toward him a little and pressed a sweet kiss against Alex's lips.

"I dreamed of this, too."

Alex said nothing. What could he say that would be enough?

That would match the feeling that poured over him like a landslide, sweeping him away.

"Kiss him again, Ben." Tristan pleaded. "I want to see it."

Ben pressed their mouths together, greedily licking his way inside past Alex's lips. His tongue delved in and caressed Alex's in a gentle, but hungry motion that made Alex moan. He reached for Ben and a warm, gentle hand wrapped around his cock.

Alex flinched and Tristan's soft laughter lilted in the quiet, dancing out between puffs of ragged breathing.

Ben pulled him in again, but this time his hands roamed over Alex's body. An onslaught of sensation, from his mouth that Ben hungrily kissed, to his dick that Tristan squeezed in a tight channel with his own, Alex got lost in it. There was no room to think of anything but the moment. Everything beyond the feel of them, and the carnal thrum of need building inside him, disappeared.

Ben pulled away and shifted, straddling Tristan's face. Alex's dick twitched in Tristan's hand at the sight of Ben sitting on his face. Ben's expression was joy and ecstasy and yet, somehow, still a burning need as he reached for Alex once more. This time with a renewed lust, driven by the tongue lapping at his hole.

Alex grabbed him and yanked him close, smashing their mouths together. Tristan jacked himself along with Alex in his hand. The glide was rough and slightly slick with precum and so much better than anything Alex had ever felt.

Ben clung to Alex like he might fly away if he didn't and Alex reached for his cock, wrapping his free hand around it as he gave a gentle tug. Ben bucked in his grip.

"Fuck. Fuck, that's." Ben panted and leaned into Alex for support. "God. Fuck." Ben whimpered and Alex had to kiss him again. His own desire, lust, satisfaction, whatever it was at that moment, careened down on him. It collapsed his world to a single point, folding all the pleasure and ecstasy in on him until he was writhing and bucking in Tristan's hand. He ground against him, kissing Ben like it was the last thing he'd do on this planet.

And then he was coming. With a yell that Ben smothered with his kiss and a jerking motion that felt too amazing, too good, too much, he coated Tristan's cock and hand with his cum, and Tristan kept stroking though Alex's cock was over sensitive now, he let Tristan drive him to the edge of insanity.

Ben rested his head on Alex's shoulder and sucked in a few heavy breaths. "Fuck, that's hot babe. Fuck. Fuck yourself with his cum. That's it." Ben spit in his hand and wrapped it around his cock, which Alex had let go of at some point, oblivious to anything but the blinding pleasure of his own orgasm.

Then Ben was coming, rocking back on Tristan's face as he came on Tristan's stomach. Finally, Tristan released Alex's cock, and he sighed happily, then Ben leaned down and in one fluid motion, he took Tristan's cock down into his mouth.

It was over in a nanosecond. Alex hadn't caught his breath before Tristan was thrusting and jerking into Ben's mouth. Alex smoothed his fingers through Ben's hair, compelled to keep touching them, to keep being a part of this, whatever it was, whatever it meant. He only knew that he wanted it.

Ben carefully rolled off Tristan and flopped onto his side. Tristan looked up at Alex with an expression of satisfied joy. He extended his hand, reaching for Alex.

"Come here." Tristan whispered, his chest heaved as he caught his breath.

Alex collapsed in a heap next to Tristan. He laid his head on Tristan's shoulder and closed his eyes when Tristan kissed his forehead. The bed wobbled and dipped a bit and then Ben was curled up with them too, on the other side of Tristan. Alex opened his eyes, and found himself staring into Ben's.

Part of Alex wanted to ask what things had been like with Eric, but he knew that comparison was the thief of joy. Not only that, but Alex knew Eric had more going for him than Alex did.

Ben reached out and with his index finger, he gently bopped the end of Alex's nose. "Whatever you're thinking, don't."

Alex scowled, caught between annoyance and appreciation that Ben had read him so easily.

"We had incredible orgasms together," Ben continued. "You have no reason to look like we kicked your puppy."

"Alex?" Tristan whispered, his voice shy and unsure suddenly. "You're okay, right?"

Alex took a breath and looked up at Tristan. "I'm okay. It's a lot, sometimes, you know. Believing all this is real."

Tristan's fingers trailed up and down Alex's side. "It's real." Tristan said. "I promise it is."

Alex had never been the type to kiss and cry, but he found himself oddly emotional about everything. He forced a smile and pulled away, hoping his happiness hid the way his doubts slammed into his heart like a battering ram.

"I need to clean up. I'll be right back." Alex untangled himself from Ben and Tristan and slipped out of the room. Once the bathroom door shut, he turned the tap on and splashed cold water onto his face.

If Ben and Tristan had guessed at his emotional turmoil, they'd let him slip out of the room to collect himself. Alex dried his face on a towel, then glanced at himself in the mirror.

He truthfully never knew what Tristan had seen in him the first time they'd been together, and it was an even bigger mystery now. Alex was plain, and his life was a mess, but Tristan wanted him here, in the perfect life he'd built with his husband, Ben.

And Ben. Fucking Ben. Alex ran his hands through his hair, then grabbed a washcloth and soaked it with hot water. He cleaned himself off and thought about Ben. Sometimes Alex believed Ben wanted him for his own reasons, and other times doubt whispered at him that Ben was only humoring Tristan and in the long run, this obligatory humoring of his husband would end and they would cast Alex aside.

Alex rinsed the cloth and got it warm again, then took it back to the room. Tristan and Ben shared a worried glance when Alex returned to the room.

Feeling awkward, Alex padded over to the bed and sat down. He handed the cloth over, feeling sheepish, strange, and out of place.

Tristan took the cloth and tidied himself, then tangled his fingers together with Alex's.

"We're glad you're here, Alex."

"I'm glad I'm here, too." Alex whispered. He felt fragile, as if they could wipe his existence out with a single word.

"But?" Ben said. He'd moved in next to Tristan, but reached out and put his hand on Alex's thigh.

Alex shrugged and sighed. "I don't know," he lied. The truth was on the tip of his tongue. He could tell them now that he wasn't good enough, but he didn't want them to agree. And he didn't want them to disagree, but have it be a lie. Both would kill him.

"But so many bad things have happened that you're afraid of having something good happen?" Ben questioned.

Alex lifted his gaze and shrugged a shoulder. "You're not wrong."

"Alex." Tristan shifted on the bed and wrapped his arms around Alex, drawing him into an embrace. He cradled him against his body as though he were this precious thing that Tristan wanted to look after. Alex hated that it was necessary for Tristan to look after him. He'd been independent once. He'd had his life together and for a few brief moments in time, he'd been a man worthy of someone like Tristan.

"Alex," Tristan repeated. "You get to have good things, too. There's so much, so much, good waiting for you, Alex. For us." Tristan pressed a kiss against Alex's shoulder.

Alex wrapped his arms around Tristan and wished he could believe it. Alex closed his eyes until someone cupped his cheek.

He opened them to see Ben staring at him, his eyes soft and warm, his expression sweet, and perhaps a little sad.

"Stay in here tonight, Alex." Ben said.

Tristan's embrace tightened. "Please," he said.

Alex was powerless to refuse these two men. "Yeah," he said. "Okay."

22

BEN

"Do you mind if I borrow your boyfriend?" Maggie asked Ben, who still hadn't shaken the cobwebs out of his brain. Last night had been amazing, and even better than the sex (which had been pretty fucking amazing) was that the three of them laid awake and whispered in the dark. They'd talked about how old times between Tristan and Alex, and Alex shared a little of what his life had been like when he lived in California.

"That depends on what you want him for." Ben smirked.

"My little sister, Vanessa, is setting up a custom t-shirt shop."

"Like tie-dye?"

Maggie snorted. "No, like silk screen." Maggie waved a hand. "Anyway, she wants to set up a website, something really nice. I showed her what Alex did with the bookstore so she wants to talk to him."

"So, talk to him. I don't own him, Maggie. He's a free agent. But I didn't know your sister was starting a business, that's really cool. Isn't she still in high school?"

Maggie nodded. "She wants to save money for art school."

"You know, I wouldn't be against ordering custom shirts from her for us to wear in the bookstore. She could do whatever she wanted on the back, something book themed maybe, but with the bookstore name on the front. Think she'd be up for it?"

"Hell yes."

"And if she had some business cards made, we can put them up by the cash register."

Alex appeared from the back of the store, Ben's old digital camera in hand. "I think I have all the shots I need. We should be able to launch the site as soon as I upload these."

Maggie leaned on the counter and rested her chin in her hand. "Alex, would you have time today at around three to talk to my sister about a website job? She wants to launch this custom t-shirt business to save money for college."

"At three?" Alex frowned. "I can't today at three, I'm looking at apartments today."

"What for?" Ben asked. Both Alex and Maggie stared at him.

"I think there's some dusting to do." Maggie said as she slipped away.

Alex looked sheepish and nervous. Ben wanted to backtrack his surprised comment, but he felt blindsided. Of course, he shouldn't, it had been the plan all along, but somehow, now that he was with him, Ben had expected him to stay with them.

"I'm sorry." Alex said. He exhaled and wrapped his arms around himself.

"I shouldn't have assumed you'd be staying. It's my fault. We never talked about plans changing. I shouldn't have assumed."

Alex shrugged. "It was the plan."

"I know." Ben took a deep breath. He didn't want Alex to leave. He liked having him around and he fit with them. After the initial bout of awkwardness, he'd slotted right into place and it was like he'd always been there. "You don't have to leave, Alex."

Alex shook his head. "It was the plan. You two were only helping me get back on my feet. And I finally have enough saved that I can."

Ben bit his lip. He wanted to pin Alex against the wall until he agreed not to leave, but he was a grown man and had to make his own decisions.

"Does Tristan know?"

Alex shook his head.

"He's going to be crushed."

Alex exhaled a long, slow breath. "I know, but… this was the plan."

"Plans can change."

Alex shook his head. "Please, don't argue with me. I need to do this."

Ben took a deep breath. "Okay. I won't stand in the way of something you say you need to do, but please know that you don't have to leave. Tristan and I love having you around."

Tristan and I love you. The sentiment was there, poured into the words Ben said in their place, because a mid-morning love confession in a bookstore wasn't the most romantic thing in the world. Nor did he want Alex to feel manipulated.

"Before you decide anything, please at least talk to Tristan and I about this, okay?" Ben went to Alex and pulled him into an embrace. "We're in this together, Alex. The three of us. I know you're used to being on your own, and making your decisions without input from anyone else, but you don't have to do that anymore. You don't have to do everything yourself. Think about it, okay?"

Alex nodded and slid his arms loosely around Ben's waist. "I will."

Ben let him pull away and watched as he went to Maggie and talked with her for a few minutes. Maggie grinned and talked animatedly with her hands, then pulled her phone out of her pocket and handed it to Alex.

Ben considered telling Tristan about Alex's plans to go apartment hunting, but he wasn't sure if that would be a betrayal or not. On one hand, Tristan deserved to know what Alex was doing, but on the other, Ben knew the information should come from Alex.

Torn, Ben tapped out a quick text to Tristan telling him he loved him. He didn't know what else to say. He felt as though Alex had thrust him into an impossible position. Ben busied himself so he wouldn't think about it, but the thoughts churned in his stomach, making him feel queasy.

It was a while before Alex found him again. Ben had holed up in his office and had sat mindlessly clicking through work he should be doing. A soft knock on the door grabbed Ben's attention and Alex stepped inside.

"Are you mad?" Alex said.

Ben took a breath. "Not mad. I'm torn. On one hand, I need us all to be on the same page. And we're not. And normally, I'd get there by telling Tristan what's going on. But this time, I can't. You need to tell him tonight, Alex."

Alex nodded. "I know. I honestly didn't think it would come as a shock, that's all. I mean," he rubbed at his chest. "I'll talk to him tonight. I promise." Alex walked closer to Ben. He hesitated, then closed the distance between them.

"I never meant to hurt you or put you in an awkward position. I'm used to doing things on my own. That's all."

Ben put his hand on Alex's hip and tugged him closer. "I know. But you don't have too anymore. And Tristan and I, we're a team, and now you're part of that team, Alex."

Ben stood and kissed Alex. It took Alex a few moments to give into the brush of Ben's lips against his, but eventually, Ben got rewarded with a gentle return of his affection. Alex was strong, but soft, and Ben could feel that he wanted to be independent, but for what reason? Was it important to him, or was it something he was used to? Ben hadn't been alone in a while, he'd had Tristan to lean on for years now, but he remembered what it had been like in the early days, how hard it had been sometimes to let go of the need to do everything himself.

"I know it's a lot to get used to, but you're not alone anymore." Ben brushed his nose against Alex's jawline. "And if it's really important to you, Tristan and I will help you find a place, but please know that you don't have to go."

Alex tensed, but made a noise of agreement before dropping his head down onto Ben's shoulder. Ben thought Alex might say something, but he pulled away and pasted a lop-sided smile on his face. "I have to get going, but I'll see you at home."

"Did you need a ride? I can wait around for you. Or pick you up?"

Alex shook his head. "I'll get an Uber."

"Tristan starts night shift soon." Ben blurted. "We should go out sometime, the two of us."

Alex blinked at him. "Like a date?"

"Yes, like a date. You and me and something fun. Something not dinner. We eat together all the time."

"Like what?"

"I don't know. What do you like to do?"

Alex leaned against the doorframe and tucked his hands into his pockets. He looked down at the floor, as if embarrassed. "I don't know. That's stupid, I get it. But I've spent so long grinding away at my job and trying to keep my head above water." Alex stopped talking and straightened up. "Whatever you decide will be fine."

"We can—"

"I'm going to be late." Alex's smile didn't hide the pain in his eyes. Something was bothering him, Ben could tell, but he didn't know what. And Alex had somewhere to be.

"Okay. I'll see you at home. Call me if you need that ride."

Alex nodded, then slipped out of the office. Ben sighed and dropped his head into his hands. He took a deep breath and his phone buzzed. Ben lifted his head and looked at the screen.

It was a message from Tristan saying he wasn't busy if Ben

wasn't busy. Ben called him and leaned back in the chair and closed his eyes when Tristan answered.

"Hey, babe," Tristan's voice was like a balm on his soul. Ben wished they were at home in bed so he could curl up against Tristan and breathe him in.

"Hey."

"What's wrong?"

"Nothing," Ben lied. He hated lying to Trisan. It made him sick to his stomach, and he walked it back. "I think something's up with Alex."

"Oh? Like what? Is he okay?"

"He seems okay, but... do you think he's too hard on himself?"

Tristan snorted. "Of course, he's too hard on himself." Something crackled in the background. "Shit, gotta call babe. See you later. Love you."

"Love you," Ben said, though the line had already gone dead. Ben leaned forward and folded his arms on his desk and dropped his head down on top of them. He took a deep breath, then another, and a third, before he pushed himself to his feet.

Ben wanted to kick his own ass for not being honest with Tristan. But between calls at work was not the time to tell Tristan that Alex was out apartment shopping. Ben worried about how Tristan would take that. He was so totally in love with Alex, even if he hadn't yet admitted it to Alex, or himself.

Maybe they should have been clearer when they talked about him being their boyfriend. Maybe they should have laid it out that they wanted him to stay with them permanently. But Tristan and Ben hadn't discussed it either. Ben had just assumed. And if he'd assumed, Tristan had likely jumped to the same conclusion.

The whole thing had quickly become a fucking mess. Ben stood and pocketed his phone. Things weren't fucked up yet. It would take a few conversations, but they'd be back on track in no time. Maybe it wouldn't even take a few conversations. All they had to do was be honest with each other. Neither Ben nor Tristan wanted Alex to leave.

Ben wondered if Alex wanted to leave, or if he felt he had to. Was it obligation that had him suddenly apartment hunting or something else? Fear, maybe? Ben couldn't stop his speculations from swirling in his mind.

He grabbed his jacket and slipped out of the store, waving to Maggie as he went. Instead of going home to an empty house, Ben climbed into the car and drove. He refused to believe that bringing Alex in had been a mistake. Nothing about his presence had felt wrong or out of place. And that was the problem. He fit so well that Ben couldn't imagine him not being there.

Somehow, Ben had fallen for him, and the idea of him leaving, even down the street or across town, was a kick in the chest.

23

TRISTAN

A domestic dispute. A heart attack. And a single vehicle collision involving a light standard and a motorcycle. Tristan was ready for the day to be over. He wanted his men, a beer, and bed, in that order. Or any order that got him naked and sandwiched between Ben and Alex the fastest.

Tristan pulled into the driveway and entered the house. "Honey, I'm home," he called out as he toed out of his shoes. He unzipped his jacket. "Honey, I'm home."

"I heard you the first time." Ben called from the kitchen.

Tristan followed the sound of Ben's voice. "Something smells amazing. Where's Honey Number Two? That's why I said it twice." Tristan padded over to the stove and lifted the lid of a pot to see spaghetti sauce. "Fucking score."

"Alex is in his room putting the finishing touches on a couple projects."

Tristan put the lid back on the sauce. "Do I have time for a shower before dinner? I've had the worst day and I want to forget it all happened."

"Of course, you do." Ben came up behind Tristan and wrapped his arms around him. "Do you want to talk about it?"

Tristan shrugged. "Not really. It can be a shitty job. Even though I love it. It's hard to watch people suffer with pain and fear. It hits different sometimes."

Ben brushed a kiss against the back of Tristan's neck. "I'm sorry you had a rough day. Take all the time you need, love."

Tristan turned in Ben's arms and relaxed. He hummed with pleasure when Ben stroked his hands up and down Tristan's back. "Too bad you can't join me in the shower. I need someone to wash my back."

"Take Alex with you," Ben suggested, kissing Tristan quickly before untangling them so he could get back to preparing dinner.

"Mmm. I better not. He's too tempting. We might miss dinner."

Ben winked at him. "Dinner will keep. Take your time."

Tristan kissed Ben again, because he could, and set off down the hallway. He stopped at Alex's closed bedroom door and knocked.

"Come in."

Tristan pulled his shirt off over his head, then opened the door. "Hey."

Alex was sitting on his bed, looking at his computer screen. He closed the laptop when Tristan came in and lifted his gaze. Tristan smiled at the way Alex's eyes widened at the sight of him.

"I'm going to have a shower. You want to wash my back for me?" Tristan leaned against the door frame and waited for an answer. "Ben said we have time before dinner."

Slowly, Alex got up and came over to Tristan. He reached for Tristan, but hesitated, so Tristan moved closer and slid his arm around Alex's waist. He buried his face in the crook of Alex's neck. "Shower with me." Tristan was bone weary from the day he'd had, and it made him feel needy. He craved being wrapped in warm arms and held and kissed and soothed. "Please."

"Yeah."

Tristan felt immediately lighter at Alex's words. Logically, he knew that having a shower couldn't wash away the day he'd had. Some days he'd lived through, he'd remember forever. But today he wanted something good to remember with all the bad.

He tugged Alex into the master bath and started the shower, then popped the button of his jeans open. He pushed them down and kicked them aside before stepping under the spray.

"Don't waste any time, do you?" Alex said.

Tristan turned and slicked his already wet hair back and watched Alex strip out of his clothes. Sometimes it hit Tristan how close he'd come to losing Alex the day of the fire. If the day had gone differently, they'd be mourning his passing instead of falling in love with him.

Tristan laced his fingers behind his head and watched Alex strip out of his pants. He was quiet today, Tristan thought, but he didn't mind. Alex had always had a busy mind, and sometimes it made him pull into himself a little.

Alex looked up and Tristan thrust his hips, his cock swayed heavy between his legs and Alex's face broke into a grin. He shook his head and stepped into the shower. His arms slid around Tristan's waist and he kissed Tristan gently, sweetly. It was a kiss that felt like home, comfort, love, all wrapped up in a bundle of promises.

Tristan wrapped his arms around Alex and turned him, pressing him into the wall. He licked his way into Alex's mouth and rutted up against him, grinding his cock against Alex. Alex made a little sound, something happy, Tristan thought, and he kissed him harder, deeper. He needed this escape, this mind-blowing, earth-moving intimacy. Sometimes Tristan thought he'd lose his mind, he was so in love with Ben, and then Alex came along again, and Tristan knew he was completely, hopelessly in love with them both.

Tristan cupped Alex's ass in his hands and rocked into him.

The rush of water made the friction slightly smoother between them and Tristan chased his release.

"You drive me wild, Alex." Tristan nipped at Alex's neck. "I'm so glad you're here."

Alex's rhythm stuttered, but Tristan pressed on. He reached a hand between them and gripped them tight in his fist.

"One day soon, I want you to fuck me. Fuck me and come in me. I can't think of anything else, Alex."

"Tristan," Alex groaned and Tristan slanted their mouths together.

Tristan wanted Alex to know then how much it meant to him, how much he meant to him.

"I love you," he said. He pulled away and blinked water out of his eyes and stared into Alex's startled gaze. "I fucking love you, Alex. I don't think I stopped."

Then, because Tristan couldn't bear it if Alex didn't say it back, he didn't give him a chance. He kissed him again, wrapping a hand around the back of his neck, greedily pinning their mouths together. He stroked them until Alex held tight to Tristan, his fingers dug into Tristan's arms as he trembled and shook apart, crying out into Tristan's mouth.

Tristan came a moment later. His grip slick with Alex's cum, he stroked them until Alex hissed and pulled away. Tristan kept a hold of his own cock for another moment, savoring the hypersensitive sensation.

"And here I thought you wanted someone to wash your back." Alex laughed and turned to face the spray of the water. The spray erased all traces of their orgasm and Tristan frowned at that. How easy it was, he thought, to wash someone away.

"You okay?" Alex asked. He squirted an ample amount of body wash on a loofah and then slid in behind Tristan. He washed him with small gentle circles and didn't demand that Tristan answer his question. Nor did he respond to Tristan's declaration. Not that he had to. If it wasn't something Alex felt yet, Tristan wouldn't force it. He wanted to hear it when Alex was ready to say it. Not out of obligation or pity or duty.

Tristan stepped out of the shower first and toweled off. Clad in only a towel, he stepped into his room and quickly slid into a pair of loose cotton pants and a worn-thin band tee. He grabbed similar clothes for Alex and returned to the bathroom.

"Here. You can wear these."

"Thanks." Alex had finished drying and stepped into the clothes while Tristan watched. He tugged the shirt down, covering his stomach. "Like what you see?" he asked.

"You look good in my stuff. You always did." Tristan grabbed Alex's hand and tangled their fingers together. "Come on, I bet dinner's ready and I seem to have worked up an appetite."

Alex snorted. "I can't imagine how that happened."

Tristan and Alex returned to the kitchen to find their small table set for three. A plate of freshly toasted garlic bread sat in the middle, and Ben brought over two plates piled high with spaghetti before returning for his own.

Tristan grabbed a slice of toast and bit into it. If they were all eating the same thing, it wouldn't matter if he had garlic breath later. "So, Alex and I were talking in the shower." Tristan dipped the edge of his toast in his spaghetti sauce. "I think we should all get tested."

Ben's fork paused in midair, and he looked at Alex, then back at Tristan. "I'd like that." Ben's fork resumed the path to his mouth, but gave Alex another strange look.

"What is it?" Tristan asked. "If you don't like the idea, or think I'm moving too fast, you can tell me. I can take it." Tristan smiled. It wouldn't be the end of the world and it would happen one day, Tristan was sure of it.

"I like the idea," Alex admitted softly. "Of being with you both, like that."

"Maybe one day soon you can move your stuff into the main bedroom with us." Tristan went on. He thought he might be getting ahead of himself by the look on Ben's and Alex's face, but he pasted on a smile. anyway. "Like, it's something to think about. We'll keep the spare room, of course, because sometimes it's nice to have some of your own space, but it would be great to wake up next to both of you every day."

Ben smiled, but his gaze cut away to meet Alex's. Tristan sucked in a breath he suddenly didn't have room for. His chest felt tight, and he looked at the two men he sat with again.

"What's going on?" Tristan asked.

Ben put his hand on Tristan's leg. "Tell him."

Tristan looked at Alex, who stared at him, gaping like a fish. "Tell me what?"

Alex rolled his shoulders back and sat a little straighter. He forced a smile onto his face and looked Tristan in the eyes. "I looked at an apartment today."

The words were a bomb that detonated in Tristan's chest. "Why?" he hated the way he wheezed the word out. The way his stupid heart cracked because he'd done it again. Hadn't he? Tristan set his fork down and stared at Alex, not understanding anything. They'd just fucked in the shower. He'd let Tristan babble on about going bare, and he hadn't said a word when Tristan said he loved him.

Of course, he didn't.

"You're leaving."

"Wasn't that the plan? You guys gave me a place to stay until I could afford to move out. I finally saved enough."

Tristan pressed the heels of his hands to his eyes until he saw stars. Until the pressure forced his tears away. He took a breath he hoped would steady him, but didn't.

"You don't need to leave, Alex. You can stay here, with us. I want you here. Ben wants you here. We're... we're together." Tristan's stomach clenched at how silent the room was.

"I know, but the plan."

"The plan involves three people now, Alex. Ben, you, and me."

He counted them off on his fingers, one at a time. "Three of us live here. There's three of us in this relationship now. It's not just you anymore."

"That's what I tried to tell him this afternoon," Ben said. He gave Tristan's leg a reassuring squeeze. Tristan dropped his hand down and covered Ben's.

Tristan was angry and hurt. And scared. It was like the first time Alex left all over again, and Tristan didn't think he could bear it. He knew he was being stupid, but it felt like Alex was already leaving them. Like this was the first step. Get one foot out the door and then he'd leave like the last time.

Tristan nodded. "I'm ah… not hungry," he cleared his throat past the knot that stuck there. He looked at Alex. "You don't have to go." Tristan stood and gave him a long look. "But like last time, I can't make you stay."

Something flashed in Alex's eyes, and he reached for Tristan. "I'm not leaving you, Tris."

"You say you're not leaving, Alex, but you're looking for apartments behind my back. You say you're not leaving, but are you staying?"

When Alex didn't respond, Tristan nodded sadly. "I need some air." He padded down the hallway and retrieved his wallet, keys, and phone from the pocket of his discarded pants.

Ben met him at the front door and they slipped out onto the front step together. Closing the door between themselves and the heavy silence inside.

"Where are you going?" Ben asked. "I can come with you… if you want. I don't want you alone right now."

"He really looked at an apartment?" Tristan hated the way his voice cracked, betraying how hurt he felt. "I feel stupid for caring. It's not like he wants to move across the country. But I won't beg him to stay, Ben." Tristan swiped at a tear that had the audacity to escape. "I did that once and I'm not a fan."

Ben cupped Tristan's face in his hands, he erased evidence of Tristan's tears with a swipe of his thumb.

"I'll talk to him."

Tristan shook his head. "Don't bother. Alex always does what he wants." Tristan leaned in and kissed Ben. He almost took him up on his offer to come with him, but a small part of him hoped Ben could get Alex to see reason.

"I'm not sure I want you driving around right now." Ben's face creased with worry. "You're upset."

Tristan nodded. "I'll be okay. I'll drive down to the park around the corner, okay?"

Ben kissed him. "And you'll call if you need me to come down there."

Tristan nodded. "And I'll call if I need you to come down there."

When Tristan arrived at the park a minute later, he sent Ben a quick text to let him know he'd arrived safely and was going to sit and watch the ducks. But it wasn't long before the car felt small and stifling. Tristan got out and wandered along the shore of the pond. And if the sun shimmering off the surface made his eyes water, well, that was okay.

24

ALEX

Ben followed Tristan outside and for a minute Alex thought they'd both left him here, staring at a table set for three, suddenly empty except for himself.

Then the front door shut and Ben appeared, a dark storm of an expression. His arms were crossed over his chest and he stared at Alex, radiating anger and hurt.

"Is he okay?" Alex asked. He shook his head because he knew it was a stupid question.

"You've broken his heart, you know that. He's sitting here talking about moving you into the bedroom with us, wanting to plan a future with you. And you were out apartment hunting like you can't get away from him fast enough."

Alex flinched at the harsh tone to Ben's words. Deep down he'd known this, that Ben would stick up for Tristan no matter what. They were husbands, that's what they did. Alex didn't hate Ben for it, but he hated the jealousy that stabbed at his guts.

"And you." Ben continued, taking a step forward. "Would it kill you to let go and allow yourself to be happy for a change?"

"What?" Alex gaped at Ben. His cheeks burned as if he'd been struck.

"You know, I get it, Alex. I really do." Ben's tone softened a little, but he kept his distance. "On one hand, you want to be this independent person. Someone who looks after himself. Someone who can stand on his own two feet. I get that. I do. When my uncle died and handed me a new life, I felt a lot of guilt. Here's all this stuff my Uncle had built for himself, and he hands it to me. Not anyone else in my family, no matter how much they might have struggled. Me. And what did I do to earn it? To deserve it?" Ben took a breath and ran a hand down his face. "I didn't do a fucking thing, Alex. Not one, to earn any of this. Now, let me ask you? Do you think I should have it?"

"Of course, it's yours. Why would you pass by something like that?"

Ben arched an eyebrow at Alex. "Do you understand, Alex? That we can have good things, even if we think we did nothing to earn them?"

Alex dropped heavily into a chair at the table. "It makes me feel small." Alex wrapped his arms around his torso to hold himself together. The weight of all his poor decisions sat on his chest, pressing the air out of his lungs, starving him of oxygen. "I'm not equal in this, Ben. There's you and Tristan, and this is all yours. And I have nothing."

Ben nodded and pulled a chair close to Alex's. "You have a history with Tristan that I will never have. And in that regard, we'll never be equal. I'll never know the younger Tristan. I'll never be his first love. I'll never have a lot of things that the two of you share. And you and I, we have a connection. At least I think so," Ben said. "A connection because we know what it's like to be alone. To have no one. To have nothing. Tristan's never lacked the love of a family. He's never known what it's like to have parents who tolerate you instead of love you. And I'm glad he'll never know those things."

Ben scooted his chair closer. "We're all equals, Alex. Not one of us is better or more important than the other. We all bring different things to this, Alex. And it's fine if a house and a fancy car and a flashy lifestyle aren't what you bring. You brought life and laughter, game nights and nostalgia. You brought a spark to Tristan's eye. And I'd be lying if I said you didn't bring something for me, Alex. Something tender and sweet and new. Something precious."

Alex loosened his hold on his torso and Ben tugged him close in an awkward hug. "How bad did I fuck up?"

"It's fixable." Ben kissed the side of Alex's head. "I want to talk to Tristan; see how he's doing. I'm going to drive over to the park and get him, okay. You hang tight." Ben pulled away only enough to brush a tender kiss against Alex's lips.

"I really want it, I do. All the things Tristan talked about. The testing and… being with you two, for real, you know. Sharing everything."

The corner of Ben's eyes crinkled, and his gaze softened. "I do, too. And everything means everything, Alex. No more sitting on your feelings. No more living in your head, talking yourself into doing things with everyone's best interests in mind without discussing it with us. I know we don't talk about Eric a lot, but part of what went wrong is that we were all shit at communicating. Eric knew we were engaged when we met, and he said he was okay with it. But once it because clear that we were going through with the wedding, he bailed. He didn't think we would, and he didn't want to feel like a third wheel, or like the odd one out."

"I like that you're married." Alex admitted.

Ben graced Alex with a smile. "Good, because I intend to stay that way."

"It makes me happy to know that Tristan has someone."

"He has two someone's. And so do I. And so do you." Ben kissed Alex on the forehead and stood. "I'll be back as soon as I can."

Ben held his gaze, and he cupped Alex's cheek. "We like

having you here, Alex. I promise we do. We wouldn't lie to you about anything, especially that. Ultimately, leaving is your choice, Tristan and I both know that. I think it's safe for me to speak for both of us and say we hope you choose to stay. We hope you want to be here as much as we want to have you here."

Alex quickly pressed his mouth against Ben's. He didn't look to deepen the kiss and search for heat and passion. What he really wanted was comfort. He wanted safety. And love. His heart was so full of wanting things that sometimes he didn't think he had room for much else.

"I need to talk to Tristan." Ben kissed the corner of Alex's mouth. "Don't go anywhere. Please."

Alex shook his head. "I promise I'll be here."

Ben nodded, then took a deep breath. A moment later he left.

Alex pressed the heels of his hands against his eyes until the pressure made the fiery burn of unshed tears fade out. The only sound he heard was the gentle hum of the fridge. Alex looked at the table and eyed all the untouched food.

He stood and took the plates to the counter. After a minute of searching in the cupboards, he found a casserole dish about the right size to hold the contents of the plates.

There was no reason all that food should go to waste. He grated cheese on top and popped it into the oven to melt it and keep it warm. When Ben came home with Tristan, they'd sort everything out and hopefully the night wouldn't be a total disaster.

After that, Alex scrubbed the dishes clean instead of loading them into the dishwasher. He needed to keep busy, or he'd go insane waiting for Ben and Tristan to come home. Without them, the house felt too big and too empty.

Alex wandered from room to room, taking in the deathly silence of the place. This is what it would be like, he realized, if he left. Sure, he'd have his own bills to pay and his own bed to sleep in. His own kitchen to cook his single meals in. But he'd also have endless stretches of silence. He'd have nothing but his own thoughts for company. Because he doubted he could leave Tristan again without Tristan giving up on him completely.

If he hadn't already.

Fuck. Alex exhaled. Why the hell didn't Ben and Tristan have a pet? Alex thought, somewhat randomly. Then he would at least have someone to talk to right now. Without Ben and Tristan, Alex's life was empty. He'd left few friends behind when he came back here, and what friends he used to have here had all disappeared, one by one.

That Ben and Tristan were not only the center of his universe, but his whole social circle disturbed Alex. He needed to get out more. He needed to make friends. But he didn't know how. All he knew was working and scraping by. Life had locked him into a survival mindset for so long he wasn't sure how he could snap out of it.

But he wanted to. More than having people to depend on, he wanted to be that for Alex and Ben. Right now, though. That clearly wasn't him. Tristan had held his heart out to Alex, and he had all but slapped it out of his hands and stomped on it.

"What the fuck did you do, Alex?" he asked himself out loud.

Alex walked into the room he'd come to look on as his own. It was supposed to have been a temporary thing, but Tristan and Ben were twin forces of nature that pulled him in and made him want things he thought he had no business wanting.

When he'd come here with his life in tatters and his tail between his legs, he never imagined that he'd fall back in love with Tristan. And Ben. Ben was even more unexpected than Tristan. The way they'd connected differed from the way he and Tristan connected, but no less special.

Ben was right. They didn't have to all have the same history to matter to each other. This wasn't a competition. It was a relationship between three people. And it was time Alex stopped thinking as if he were all on his own. Because he hadn't been from the moment Tristan and Ben brought him in. They'd tried their best to show him how good his life could be and how amazing they could be together.

Alex hoped he hadn't made an irreversible mistake.

25

BEN

The thought of things not working out with Alex caused a sharp pain that shot all the way through Ben, like a hot knife carving out chunks of his heart. He'd gotten attached, but Alex made it easy to care for him, in his own stubborn, stupid, selfish way.

Alex didn't mean to be selfish, Ben told himself. But he thought of how upset Tristan had been, and his stomach clenched. If things with Alex didn't work out, Ben doubted he and Tristan would ever seek out another third. A triad had been something they'd both wanted for as long as they'd known each other. Eric leaving had hurt enough.

When Ben pulled into the parking lot near the park, he'd expected to see their other car, the one Tristan had left in a little while ago. He circled the lot three times before he concluded that Tristan wasn't there. Ben pulled into a parking space and patted his pockets until he found his phone.

Instead of texting, he called. Thankfully, Tristan answered on the second ring.

"Babe," Ben exhaled. "I'm at the park. Where are you?"

"I'm at Mom and Dad's. There were too many people at the

park and I didn't want to look like an idiot if I burst into tears in front of a bunch of ducks."

"Oh, Tris."

"I'll be okay." Tristan let out a heavy sigh.

"I'll be there as soon as I can."

"I'm out at the gazebo. I didn't even go inside. I'm the worst son ever." Tristan let out a sad, self-deprecating laugh.

"You're the best son ever, and you know they love you. I'll be there in a few minutes, okay, Love?"

"Do you think he'll stay?"

Ben hated how small and sad and defeated Tristan sounded.

"I think we'll be okay even if he doesn't." Then because he needed to say it as much as Tristan needed to hear it, he added. "I love you. And him. And I'm not keen on letting him go so easily either. But I don't think he wants to leave."

"You don't?" Tristan's voice trembled hopefully.

"I don't. I'll talk to you soon, okay. Take a deep breath, hug your mom and get a glass of water."

Tristan acquiesced, and the call ended. Ben spent the drive over thinking about all the ways this day had gone sideways. It wasn't often he doubted himself and the decisions he made, but had it been smart to invest his emotions in a man Tristan had a past with? Maybe not, but falling for Alex hadn't been a conscious decision. He didn't wake up one day and say to himself, hmm, maybe I'll fall for my husband's ex today because we all need more baggage in our lives.

By the time Ben stopped the car and made his way to Bonnie and Glen's back yard, Ben was as tangled up in knots as he'd been earlier. Space from his men had done little to help, all it had done was to provide him with plenty of time to overthink everything.

He found Tristan in the gazebo. It was a large one, with space for a bench around the inside perimeter and still plenty of room in the middle for a swing. It was easy enough to remove if they wanted to have events here, like a wedding, and that's where Ben found Tristan.

He sat to one side of the swing. He braced his feet on the floor of the gazebo and rocked himself slowly. His head turned at the sound of Ben's footsteps coming up the stairs and when Ben dropped into the seat next to him, Tristan snuggled into his side.

Tristan sniffled and wiped at his face. "Sometimes, Ben. Sometimes I feel stupid."

"You're not." Ben kissed the top of Tristan's head and wrapped an arm around him, pulling him closer.

Tristan snorted. "I know I'm not. I said sometimes I feel stupid. But thank you for sticking up for me."

"I will always stick up for you."

Tristan sighed. "Do I sense a but, coming?"

Ben smiled, "But I think I understand where Alex is coming from. Not that I agree with him, but his reasons make sense to me."

Tristan shifted out of Ben's grasp enough so he could look him in the eyes. "Well, I don't. Why would he want to leave? Again? Why does he keep… running away from me? I want him, Ben, and it's like nothing I do is enough to keep him."

Ben leaned in and pressed his lips to Tristan's. "He's not running away from you, Tristan. He's running to what is familiar to him. The thing is, he's not like you, Tris." Ben paused and searched for Tristan's hand and tangled their fingers together. "He didn't have all this, the whole loving family thing. He doesn't know what it's like to have people who want him to stick around."

"He told you this?" Tristan's brow furrowed, and he looked hurt by the idea that Alex would confide in Ben, but not him. But Ben saw the ache there, too. The compassion Tristan felt for Alex, even through his own pain.

"He and I have a lot in common, Tristan. You know how my family is. I never knew how family could really be until I became a part of yours. I never knew that people would want to be there for me until your Dad got upset that I'd wait in the rain for three hours for a tow truck when I could've called him and asked for a hand changing my tire. I never knew that someone would care that I got sick and stop by my house with chicken soup because their son said I was sick. I never knew what any of that was like, and sometimes, Tristan, sometimes it scared the life out of me, because if I lost you, I'd lose all that too. You brought so much light and love into my life that sometimes I still don't know what to do with it all."

Tristan blinked at him. "I never realized." He whispered. "I love my family, but I never thought kindness could be intimidating."

"It can be, sometimes, if you're not used to being on the receiving end. And he's had a lot of bad luck, I think he's had so much bad that he has trouble trusting anything good."

Tristan pouted. "How do you know all this, and I don't?"

"Because you live in a land of endless possibilities, which is amazing, and I love you for it. It's what makes you, you. It's what breathes life and light into everything you touch. But Alex, he's been in survival mode for so long I don't think he knows how to stop himself sometimes. He didn't mean to hurt us."

"I know." Tristan leaned into Ben and gripped tighter to his hand.

"Do you?"

"Yes. I think… was I too harsh on him?"

Ben shook his head. "No, love. You weren't harsh, you were upset, and you had every right to be, but now, we have to get home and the three of us need to have a long, long chat about everything."

Tristan made no move to get up, instead he burrowed into Ben's side. "Remember when we got married?"

"Of course, I do."

"Remember how happy we were? I wanted that with him once

upon a time. I thought he was it for me, you know. And I'm glad things worked out the way they did, because I love you, Ben. I can't regret what happened. But sometimes…"

Ben clung tight to his husband. "Sometimes you wish things could've been different, despite how good they are."

Tristan looked at Ben and furrowed his brow. "You understand?"

"Sure I do, love. My family is a fractured mess. I don't talk to them because they barely tolerate my existence. They still won't refer to you as my husband half the time. And I love you, and I love the life we have together, but sometimes I wish they weren't so awful that I moved across the country at the first opportunity. Sometimes I wish they were kind and warm and that I wanted to be around them."

"Oh, Ben." Tristan's eyes filled with tears. "I'm sorry."

"You have nothing to be sorry for. I wanted you to know, so you know I understand we can wish things would've turned out differently, even though we're madly in love. Even though we love our lives. It's okay to have feelings we don't always understand, Tristan. It's okay to ache for things that didn't turn out how we wanted, even if we love our reality. Sometimes, things suck."

Tristan wiped at his eyes. "God. I'm a mess, today, Ben. I shouldn't have left, but today was too much. First…" Tristan's voice caught, and he cleared his throat. "First we lost someone today. I couldn't bring him back, Ben. I tried and tried, but he… he gave up. And then I got home and without even talking to you about it first, I wanted Alex to move into the master with us. I couldn't stand the thought of going without both of you for even a second."

"I'm sorry you had a shitty day."

"I'm sorry I didn't talk to you about it sooner." Tristan wiped at his face again. "Can we go home?"

"Absolutely." They stood and exited the gazebo hand in hand

and made their way slowly to their cars. "Did you want to ride with me? I can come for the car before work tomorrow?"

"I'll be okay. A few minutes alone to compose myself might be a good idea." Tristan pecked Ben on the lips, then pulled away. "I'll be right behind you."

Tristan started toward his car, then stopped and turned to Ben. "What if he wants to leave?"

"Then we let him. But I don't think he wants to leave, so let's go home and let him know why we want him to stay."

"I love him, Ben."

"I know you do. I do, too."

Tristan's mouth finally twitched and attempted to smile. "Good. I'm glad."

Ben unlocked his car and with a last look of longing at his husband, they climbed into their cars and headed home, hoping to find Alex still there. He might have already left, Ben told himself. He pictured a thousand different scenarios on the way home, and the only one he couldn't stand was the one where Alex hadn't stayed.

But Ben walked into the house and saw Alex's coat on the hook and his shoes lined up by the door. His heart gave a happy flutter. If Alex was here, they had a chance. Tristan walked in a second later and toed his shoes off. He lined them up next to Alex's, then grabbed Ben's hand.

"Here goes nothing." Tristan said, then they set off in search of Alex.

26

TRISTAN

Tristan didn't know what to expect when he walked in the door, but he didn't expect Alex to be in the kitchen pulling a casserole dish out of the oven.

Alex looked at them sheepishly as he set the dish on the stovetop and pulled the oven mitts off. "I didn't want dinner to go to waste," he explained. He tucked his now empty hands in his pockets and looked down at his feet. Then up at Tristan. "I fucked up. I'm sorry."

Tristan took a deep, shaky breath. "Ben explained some things to me while we were out." Tristan dropped Ben's hand and approached Alex. A million things churned in his mind. He thought of all the different things he could've said in this moment. He mapped out various outcomes on the drive home, and the only ones that made the ache in him ease were the ones where Alex stayed. Tristan chewed on his lower lip for a second as he reached for Alex. He cupped Alex's face in his hands. "You make me feel things that scare me, Alex. I want you here with us so fucking much that it hurts. And I should have told you that. I should have told you a lot of things. We haven't been together long, but I should've told you how much you mean to me. That I didn't, that's on me. But we're in this relationship too, Alex. It's not just you. You're not alone anymore, you never have to be alone ever again. You can have us and all that comes with it."

Alex's hands came up, and he grabbed Tristan's wrists. Alex gripped him tight and his eyes fluttered shut. "I don't… I don't know what to say. I keep hurting you. I'm sorry. God, that sounds flimsy and pathetic."

Tristan pulled Alex in until their foreheads rest together. "Say you'll stay. The rest we can work through, but I can't…" Tristan swallowed around a lump of emotion. "I can't handle you leaving me again Alex. Maybe I should have fought harder for us years ago and things might have been different. Maybe you hate me for not going with you and that's why you can't trust that this will last, but Alex, I don't want you to leave. I didn't want you to go then, and I don't want you to go now. I don't care if it's a mile down the road or right next door. Don't go."

Alex's fingers tightened on Tristan's wrists. "I already called the landlord and turned the apartment down. I'd like to stay. I don't want to leave. I never did. I don't deserve any of this. My life is still a mess. I'm barely making it. I was barely making it before the fire and since then everything's been a wreck." Alex let go of Tristan's wrists, wound his arms around Tristan's waist, then he settled in close, burrowing up against Tristan as if he were seeking refuge. "I'm so tired, Tristan. I'm tired of scraping and scrounging and chasing clients down to pay their invoices. I'm tired."

Tristan smiled and because Alex couldn't see him, pressed a kiss to the side of Alex's head. His hair smelled like coconuts. "And yet you wanted to leave and keep doing everything on your own."

"I want to be worthy of you both. I want to have something to bring to this relationship."

Tristan stepped back enough to tilt Alex's face up so he could look him in the eyes. "Since when have you not been worthy? You don't need to bring things. I have things. Ben has things. What we don't have, is you. What we want, is you. We don't care if you're struggling to make it. It doesn't matter if you're not rich and famous. We care that you're happy and healthy and here."

Alex was silent for so long Tristan wondered if he'd changed his mind again and wanted to leave. He'd let him go, because that's who Tristan was, but it would hurt more than anything he'd ever felt.

"I want to stay."

Alex's confession knocked the wind out of Tristan. His knees quaked, but he stayed on his feet and he crashed his mouth down on Alex's, demanding entry with his tongue. He kissed him with the desperation of a man finding water in the desert.

Tristan pulled away long before he was ready to. "Then stay. Stay." He kissed Alex again. "Stay."

He didn't know Ben had approached until his hands settled on Tristan's waist and he felt a puff of air wash against his neck. "We don't want you to leave." Ben said, making Tristan warm all over.

"I don't want to leave." Alex finally admitted. His gaze flickered back and forth from Tristan's to Ben's. "I want to stay. I want to be with you."

"We'll all have to communicate better." Ben moved closer to Alex. He put a hand on Alex's waist and tugged him closer.

Alex swallowed. "Then, I should… maybe tell you both how much I want you. All of you. Both of you." Alex's chest rose and fell. His cheeks flushed pink and Tristan's gaze moved lower, taking in the sight of Alex's dick pressed tight against the front of his pants.

Tristan pulled Alex closer. He cupped his ass with one hand and ground his dick against Alex, showing him how fucking mutual his lust was. "Put dinner back in the oven." His voice was a husky rumble. He didn't want to wait. Wouldn't wait. He'd have Alex now, in the kitchen if he had to.

"I didn't mean now." Alex blushed but didn't protest when Ben put the casserole dish back in the oven.

"Now is perfect." Tristan kissed him again, light and sweet. He gently licked his way between Alex's lips and delved his tongue deep inside. Alex stepped closer, winding his arms around Tristan. Alex whimpered when Tristan pulled away. "Now is everything."

"I don't..."

Tristan cut him off. "Stop. If you're next words are about what you don't deserve, or don't think you deserve, I don't want to hear it."

Alex chuckled softly. He pressed his mouth against the corner of Tristan's. "I was going to say that I don't know what I'd do if you ever gave up on me."

"You'll never have to find out." Tristan made the promise as easy as breathing. "I never really got over you, Alex."

"It's true." Ben said. He came up behind Alex and settled his hand on Alex's hips.

Alex turned his head and looked at Ben. "And you don't mind?"

Ben smiled. "I fell for him knowing there was a guy out there he'd fallen so hard for that part of him still loved you. And I was okay with that because I liked the idea of loving someone that way. Of having someone love me so hard they'd love me across time and distance, through separation and struggle."

"I never want to need to learn to live without you, either of you, ever again." Tristan tugged Alex toward the bedroom. "From now on, we talk more. We talk about things, no matter how little or how big, how hard or personal. I won't keep losing people I love."

Alex blinked at Tristan. "Love?"

"Don't look so shocked, Alex. You must know how much I fucking love you. I always have. I always will. I didn't stop loving you then and I won't stop loving you now." They entered the room, and the earth stood still. Tristan took a deep breath and looked at his men and felt how lucky he was down to his bones. Some people spent a lifetime without the love he'd been lucky enough to find with not just one man, but two. "You two are it for me. There's nowhere I'd rather be, forever, than with both of you."

Ben slid Alex's shirt up, urging Alex with a quiet whisper to raise his arms. Ben cast the shirt aside and his mouth came down on the slope of Alex's neck, licking and sucking. Alex's eyes fluttered shut, and he moaned as he reached for Tristan, pulling him closer.

Alex held tight to Tristan's waist. He rocked forward when Ben sucked his earlobe into his mouth. Tristan cupped Alex's cheek and leaned in slowly. He wanted to remember this moment forever. The way Ben and Alex looked together was intoxicating. Alex's dark lashes fanned out against his cheeks, highlighting his flushed skin. Ben looked at Tristan and their gazes locked. Tristan leaned closer, cupping the side of Ben's face as he pulled him into a kiss with Alex sandwiched between them.

Alex groaned and ground his cock against Tristan.

"That's so..." Alex stopped talking when Ben bit Tristan's lower lip and tugged on it.

Tristan worked on undoing Alex's pants. "That's so what?" he asked, watching Ben turn his attentions back to Alex.

"Thank you." Alex trembled. "For not giving up on me. For loving me and for letting me in."

Ben slid his hands up Alex's chest, stopping to pinch his nipples as he sucked a bruise up on Alex's neck. "You belong with us." Ben said, sliding his hands down, urging Alex's pants down his hips. "Get him naked, love."

Tristan didn't have to be told twice. He grabbed Alex's pants, hooking his fingers into the band of his briefs and he tugged them down, smiling when Alex's cock sprang free and bobbed in air in front of him. Tristan leaned in and gave the head a flick with his tongue.

"Fuck." Alex jolted where he stood. He tried to buck forward, but Ben's hands gripped him, keeping him in place.

"Patience, sweetheart." Ben crooned in Alex's ear as Tristan tugged the pants the rest of the way down Alex's legs. He liked the sound of the endearment coming off Ben's tongue. Tristan's heart swelled in his chest with an unfamiliar warmth and brightness.

He didn't think it was possible to love Ben any more than he had, but the more Ben loved Alex, the harder Tristan fell for his husband. His capacity to care and love, to nurture and protect never ceased to amaze Tristan, but this differed from before. It had been one thing to have Ben's sole attention, but now Tristan got to be on the outside, looking in, and he liked what he saw.

He loved the way Alex melted against Ben, trusting him to be there. Tristan doubted he'd ever tire of watching Ben take Alex apart with his lips, his hands, with the way he gripped Alex tight and rocked their bodies together.

"Please," Alex said. His hand found Tristan's hair, and he tangled his fingers in it.

Tristan helped him out of his pants, one leg at a time. Once they were tossed off to the side, Tristan slid his hands up the outsides of Alex's fuzzy legs.

"What do you want, sweetheart?" Tristan asked. Alex gazed down at him, his pupils blown wide at the sight of Tristan's mouth nearing his cock.

"Please." Alex begged, giving Tristan's hair a painful tug that made Tristan hiss. "Shit, sorry." Alex's grip eased, but Tristan looked up at him.

"Don't be sorry." He took Alex's cock in hand, wrapping his fingers around the thick base. He used his other hand to grab Alex by the wrist and guide his hand back to Tristan's hair. "And don't stop."

He welcomed the harsh grip and the slight sting of pain in his scalp as he took Alex into his mouth. It grounded him, keeping him in the moment, reminding him this was real. His men were here with him, with nothing between them but love and lust and the desire for a future together.

When Alex's entire body flinched, and he leaned forward slightly. Tristan opened his eyes and pulled back until he saw why. Ben had gone to his knees behind Alex. Tristan wasted no time swallowing Alex back down until his nose pressed into the thick thatch of hair at the base of Alex's dick.

Alex keened and moaned above them, spurring them on. And when Ben's hand found one of Tristan's and laid over top of it, the moment became even more perfect than Tristan thought possible.

27

ALEX

The bed stood not four feet away, yet Alex swayed, struggling to stay on his feet as Tristan sucked him down, flattening his tongue against the underside of Alex's cock. And Ben's tongue swirled and licked and pressed inside Alex's hole. And though the bed he knew to be extremely comfortable stood mere feet away, he couldn't make himself move.

Alex had known happiness to be a spell that could be broken, and this felt no different. And yet, Tristan wanted him here. Ben wanted him here. For the first time since he left, he felt like he really belonged somewhere.

Did that scare him? Fuck yes, it did. But Tristan looked up at him, his mouth full of Alex's cock, and the love in his eyes was unmistakable. Unshakeable. Tristan loved harder and faster than anyone Alex had ever met. He'd been afraid of that love before and what it meant. He always thought he'd have to earn it somehow. Deserve it. Pay for it in sweat and tears.

But Tristan didn't want any of that. He hadn't wanted it when Alex had dreams as tall as skyscrapers. He'd wanted this. Alex realized Tristan had wanted a simple life with the man he loved.

Now he wanted the same thing, but instead of one man it was two.

Ben's fingers spread Alex's cheeks apart, and he attacked his hole again with renewed vigor, pressing his tongue through the muscle. Alex's legs shook so hard he had to brace himself on Tristan's shoulders.

"Fucking hell, Ben."

Tristan released Alex's cock with a lewd pop. His smile was bright and blinding. His eyes twinkled when he spoke, the happiness in them unable to be contained. "We should move to the bed before your legs give out."

Alex snorted. "What legs?" He jolted when Ben pressed his tongue in further. "I can't feel my legs. I can't feel my face."

Tristan stood, grimacing slightly as he got off the floor. "So dramatic." He moved closer until their bodies pressed against each other. Then he cradled Alex's face in both of his hands and kissed him.

And fucking hell, what a kiss. Alex couldn't breathe through the emotion behind it. It felt like Tristan was telling him all the things he hadn't said. The way his tongue moved inside Alex's mouth, searching and caressing. Tristan's fingers twitched and eventually made their way into Alex's hair as Tristan ground himself against Alex, their cocks bumping and sliding between them.

When Ben's tongue finally left Alex's hole, his entire body was a quivering mess. Ben kissed his way up Alex's back, peppering his spine, he kissed his way across Alex's shoulders and his hands gripped Alex by the waist.

Teeth dragged against Alex's earlobe. "What do you think, love?"

Alex reluctantly let Tristan pull away from the kiss so he could answer Ben.

"Bed," Tristan said, breathlessly. "Definitely bed. Now."

Tristan climbed onto the bed and kneeled there, motioning

for Alex to come closer. With Ben crowding him from behind, urging him forward, Alex had no choice but to follow. Not that he would have chosen differently. He needed these men like oxygen, and he let Tristan pull him closer once he climbed onto the bed.

Ben rustled around in the nightstand and dropped a handful of condoms and a bottle of lube on the bed.

"I'll get tested soon. Tomorrow." Alex promised. "I want this with both of you, so much." He reached for Ben and tugged him closer. The feelings he'd been afraid of bubbled up inside him. "I can't breathe when I'm not with you. I didn't mean for any of this to happen, but fuck. I love both of you so much." Alex sucked in a deep breath and forced himself to stop talking. If he got going, he felt like he'd never stop. His emotions and his vulnerabilities lay on the surface, and it made him feel infinitely fragile.

Ben kissed him gently and lowered him, urging him to lie flat on the bed. Then he covered Alex's body with his own. They shared a breath when their lips separated and Ben's voice rang out in the quiet, soothing Alex's fears. "I love you, Alex. I need you to know that."

Alex took a breath, and he shut his eyes, concentrating on getting the tremble in his chin to stop. "I know."

They didn't talk after that. Ben pushed Alex's arms above his head and pinned them there. He kissed a trail lower, his lips blazing trails of heat around Alex's cock, down the insides of his thighs.

Fingers tickled their way up the inside of Alex's arm, and he lifted his gaze to see Tristan towering over him. Alex's heart beat like a bass drum, thumping steady and wild.

"Open up for me, sweetheart." Tristan crooned softly, stroking Alex's cheek, sinking his thumb into Alex's mouth. Alex sucked on the digit, swirling his tongue around it, moaning at the look of pure lust on Tristan's face.

Tristan pulled his thumb free and shimmied closer. Then

closer still. The soft skin of Tristan's sac brushed down Alex's face and he flicked his tongue out, caressing the tender underside of it.

Alex closed his eyes and let the wondrous pleasure of worshipping Tristan engulf him completely. Tristan shimmied again, and parted his cheeks with his hands, lowering himself down on Alex's face.

Alex let out a throaty moan and went to work, licking and sucking and plunging his tongue into Tristan's entrance. He was so engrossed in his task that he jumped when a slick finger pressed against his hole, then dipped in, sliding all the way inside. Alex spread his legs, a wordless plea for more. He clutched at Tristan's thighs, clung tight as that finger slowly worked its way in and out. The pace agonizingly, deliciously slow. His skin felt tight and hot and the need for more pulsed in him like heat lightning flashing against a dark sky.

Alex panted against Tristan's skin. "Fuck me. Please."

The crinkle of a condom wrapper answered him before Ben or Tristan did.

"Who first?" Tristan asked, sliding off Alex, allowing him to breathe more freely.

"Don't care. Someone. Both. Either."

Tristan flopped over, a slightly ungraceful tangle of limbs and flesh. Then he was grabbing Alex and rolling him over on top of him. He wound his arms around Alex's neck and smashed their mouths together with a clack of teeth.

Tristan's impatience matched Alex's own, and he rocked and bucked, getting lost in the friction of their dicks pressed together, leaning against each other like old friends. Then Ben returned with a warm hand that ran down the length of Alex's spine and lubed fingers that breached his hole.

Whatever sound it was that Alex made, a whine, a keen, or a moan, Tristan smothered it with his kisses, swallowing it down greedily. Tristan held Alex tight against him, pinning him close as Ben worked him open.

Before long, the blunt head of Ben's cock pressed against Alex's hole. The kiss he shared with Tristan slowed, becoming less desperate as Ben pushed inside at a languid pace, allowing Alex to get used to the size of him.

Alex panted, open-mouthed, as Tristan kissed his way along his jaw, stroking his shoulders, whispering sweet nothings into his ear as Ben bottomed out, then stilled. His hands gripped Alex's hips, and he leaned forward, pressing a kiss between Alex's shoulders.

Alex shut his eyes because the world was too bright and beautiful and he almost came apart from happiness. It welled up inside him, the feeling of belonging, one he'd never felt this viscerally before.

To stave off the tears he felt stinging his eyes, he buried his face in the curve of Tristan's neck and clung tight to him.

No one had the air to speak. Or maybe, Alex thought, it affected them as it did him and they didn't dare. Some things were meant to be seen, but not touched, like soap bubbles floating on the wind. If you touched them, they'd burst. This felt like that. Like at any second, things might pop. So they didn't speak and instead they held tight to each other, chasing friction and easing their lusty urges, giving in to the pleasure of each other's flesh.

Ben shuddered and gripped Alex's shoulders. He rammed in hard, over and over again, and with a roar, he came, lurching and pulsing. Alex felt him quake as he kept going, emptying inside the condom.

Then he slowed, but kept going. This time he leaned forward again and peppered more kisses to the back of Alex's neck.

"Need you." Tristan said, bucking his hips. Alex's cock twitched in agreement and he kissed Tristan, open-mouthed and needy.

"Yes."

Ben eased out of him and got rid of the condom. He stretched out on his side. He smoothed a hand down Alex's back. "Come here." His voice was thick with emotions.

"Lay on your side, Alex." Tristan slid out from under him and reached for a condom. Alex turned his attention to Ben, who looked wrecked and emotional and sated, but still hungry, somehow. He clearly wanted more, despite having just come.

Alex laid down next to him and their legs tangled together. Ben's fingers grazed the underside of Alex's chin and he kissed him with a gentleness that took Alex's breath away.

Behind him, the bed dipped, and Tristan's warmth appeared at his back. Slick and hot and thick, he pressed his cock inside Alex's hole without pause. He wound an arm around Alex's front, pressing his hand into Alex's abdomen, his forehead pressed into Alex's back between his shoulder blades.

Ben's hand traveled down and gripped Alex's cock. Alex bucked his hips, fucking the channel Ben made with his fist.

"That's it, sweetheart. Let us take care of you."

The endearment made Alex's eyes sting again, and if a tear slipped free when Ben was kissing him, he wouldn't notice.

Tristan's pace, that started out lush and languid, hurried suddenly. "Fuck, Alex. I can't wait. I can't… oh fuck." Tristan babbled as his hips snapped. He buried himself deeper and deeper inside Alex. His open mouth pressed against Alex's shoulder. He panted and groaned, his rhythm falling apart as he came. "Fuck. Fucking. Fuckingloveyou." Tristan cried out.

Then Alex was coming too. Falling to pieces in Tristan's arms, spending himself into Ben's hand. Cradled between two men he'd grown to love completely and couldn't live without. Two men who wouldn't give up on him. Men determined to give him everything.

He didn't realize his shoulders shook until Tristan wrapped

himself around Alex like an overly friendly octopus and Ben cradled Alex against his chest. They crooned softly as he cried.

He only cried long enough to feel properly ridiculous. He wiped at his eyes and let out a weak, watery laugh. "The sex wasn't bad. I promise."

Tristan's laughter echoed his own.

"We know that," Ben assured him, gently smoothing his fingers through Alex's sweaty hair.

28

BEN

Ben scanned the crowded room for signs of his husband, or their boyfriend. Catching sight of Bonnie instead, Ben wove his way through the throng of people and made his way over to his mother-in-law.

He'd recently started calling her Mom, much to her surprise and delight. Ben had severed contact with his family after a particularly ugly phone call after Ben and Tristan updated their friends online to the status of their relationship.

It had taken him some time to adjust to not having his family in the background of his life at all, not even as an afterthought. The weight off his shoulders freed him to do things like call Bonnie and Greg, Mom and Dad.

Ben strode across the manicured lawn and sidled up next to Bonnie. "Have you seen my husband? Or my boyfriend? I've lost them somehow."

A twinkle in Bonnie's eye indicated she knew exactly what was going on. "No, dear. I haven't seen them."

Ben narrowed his gaze. "You are a terrible liar."

Bonnie laughed and patted Ben on the arm. "Yes, I am." She sipped at a bottle of water. Though it was an early summer morning, the sun pounded down on them and threatened a sweltering day. Bonnie had organized the transformation of the local soccer fields into a carnival. All proceeds going to the nearby children's hospital.

"Have you been to the dunk tanks yet, Ben?" Bonnie asked with a grin.

Ben laughed. "So that's where you hid them."

"Seemed like a good day for it. That boyfriend of yours worked his ass off helping me set this up, the least I could do was make sure he got in on the fun."

After they agreed Alex should stay with them permanently, he'd sat down and told them he didn't want them to be his only social interactions, but that he didn't know what to do.

Tristan suggested helping Bonnie with her volunteer work. Alex hit the ground running and hadn't looked back. He worked less, which both Ben and Tristan appreciated. The volunteer work got him out more and had done wonders for his self-esteem and self-worth. He'd even set up his own small program to help people, mainly youths, set up online businesses.

"This place looks great, Mom." Ben couldn't keep the affection out of his voice, and Bonnie's gaze sparkled when she looked at him.

"Thank you, Ben." Bonnie patted Ben's arm gently. "I'm glad you boys have Alex. He's been good for both of you."

Ben nodded in agreement. A knot of emotion sat thick in his throat, making it impossible to speak.

Bonnie nudged him and pointed off to the right side of the field. "The dunk tanks are over that way." She glanced at the dainty watch on her wrist. "Alex is almost done. If you want in on the fun, you'll have to hurry."

Ben bent and kissed Bonnie on the cheek and set off in search of his men. They weren't hard to find; it turned out. The dunking tanks were popular that day, with a line stretching past the face painting tent and down to where the row of food trucks started.

He spotted Alex climbing out of the dunk tank, dripping wet. Instead of climbing back up on to the platform, he climbed the ladder and got out of the tank, meeting Tristan who wrapped a large fluffy towel around him. Tristan's need to take care of everyone had endeared Ben to him from the very beginning. After years of neglect from his own family, Tristan's attentions soothed something inside Ben. Tristan made him feel wanted, loved. Worthy. It warmed Ben to see Alex melt under the same attention.

Tristan pulled Alex close and Ben watched the sweet kiss as he approached, the smile on his face widening with every step. At times his life felt surreal. Like it was a dream, and he'd wake up, panting and sweating in the dark, clinging to the last vestiges of a fading fantasy.

Ben was nearly upon them before they noticed his approach. "Sorry I'm late." His heart fluttered even as he apologized. He wished they weren't somewhere so public. He wanted to plaster himself against Alex's soaking wet body. It appeared he must have telegraphed his thoughts because Tristan met his gaze and whispered something in Alex's ear that made him turn bright red.

"Are the two of you conspiring against me?" Ben kissed Alex. He smelled fresh and wet. Water dripped from the ends of his hair.

"Conspiring? Yes." Tristan stepped closer and brushed his lips across Ben's. "Against you? Never. I assure you this conspiracy is one-hundred percent mutually beneficial."

"A mutually beneficial conspiracy?" Ben shrugged. "I think I can live with that. Is Mom done with you, Alex?" Ben asked, eyeing his wet, sexy boyfriend.

"Yeah. She said the rest of the crew could deal with take down. I need to change."

Tristan slid a black backpack containing Alex's change of

clothing off his shoulder and handed it to Alex. "We'll wait here for you."

Alex took his things and headed to the tent that served as a changing room behind the dunk tank.

When he was out of sight, Tristan leaned in. "Is everything ready?"

"Yeah. I got everything set up this morning." Ben had told Alex that he was going to be late coming to the carnival because he had to sort something out at the bookstore. In reality, he and Tristan had conspired behind his back to do something special for him. Ben hoped he liked it.

Joy radiated from Tristan. The light in his eyes drew Ben in like a siren song. Tristan glanced around before stepping closer.

"What if he says no?" Tristan had lowered his voice, but the fear in it was still apparent enough to make Ben's heart hurt for Tristan.

"He won't say no." Ben promised. "We've come a long way in the past six months. He wasn't ready before."

"And you think he is now?" Tristan bit his lower lip.

"Yeah. I think he is."

Tristan took a deep breath and raked his hand through his hair. "Okay. You're right. He's ready. We're ready. It's going to be fine."

"It will be, you'll see."

"Give me a five-minute head start." Tristan brushed a kiss against Ben's lips before he set off toward the parking lot.

Alex appeared a minute later. Ben smiled at the confused look on his face. "Where'd Tristan go?"

Ben only smiled.

Alex raised an eyebrow in response. "What are you up to?"

"If I told you, it wouldn't be a surprise."

Alex pouted. "I hate surprises."

Ben slid his arm around Alex's waist. "You'll love it. Trust me." He felt Alex sigh.

"There was no emergency at the bookstore this morning, was there?" Alex sounded like he was trying very hard to be irritated at Ben's dishonesty.

"Nope." Ben didn't mask the gleeful tone to his voice.

"And I suppose Tristan's sudden disappearance means he's also in on this."

Ben guided them toward his car. "I could tell you, but then I'd have to beat your ass in Mario Kart."

"Like you already don't? Here I thought Tristan was the one to beat, but you have no soul. There's competitive and then there's you, Mr Cackle-when-my-boyfriend-falls-off-Rainbow Road. Over and over again."

"I cannot be held responsible for my reaction to the adorable sounds you make when you get frustrated."

"I'm not adorable," Alex huffed adorably.

"Okay, you're not adorable. You're precious."

"Stop." Alex groaned, dragging the word out until his tone bordered on petulance.

"Never."

On the drive home, Alex stayed quiet. His leg bounced slightly, highlighting his nerves. Ben reached over and placed his hand on Alex's leg.

"It won't be a bad surprise, I promise."

Alex smiled. "I know." He put his hand over top of Ben's. "But you know I don't like it when you two make a fuss over me."

"We like making a fuss over you. Someone has to. You deserve it." Ben glanced at Alex, sending him a sharp, no-nonsense look. "And don't argue with me. It's not an argument you'll win."

Alex huffed, and Ben almost felt how hard Alex rolled his eyes. Ben and Tristan had spent a lot of time telling Alex how deserving he was, but they decided maybe he needed to see it. Maybe he needed proof of the things they said.

Ben pulled into the driveway and killed the engine.

Alex's seatbelt unbuckled, but he didn't move. "The surprise is here."

"It is." Ben licked his lips. His skin was tight with anticipation. It felt like Christmas day, minutes away from the grand gift-opening.

"Did you get me a puppy?" Alex raised an eyebrow and Ben laughed.

"Sorry, sweetheart. It's not a puppy. But we can discuss that if you want. But later. Come on, out you get."

Ben climbed out of the car and walked to the front door with Alex. "Go on," Ben urged.

Alex shot him a look of trepidation, but walked into the house. He stopped dead at the sight of rose petals on the floor, leading into the house and down the hallway.

Alex remained silent and carefully toed out of his shoes. He pushed them off to the side and looked back at Ben. "What's all this?"

"It's part of your surprise. I wonder where they go?" Ben watched Alex's chest expand as he sucked in a deep, fortifying breath.

"Here goes nothing." Alex said as he followed the trail of flower petals.

Ben trailed behind Alex down the hallway and paused outside the bedroom door where the rose petals led them.

Alex put his hand on the doorknob and turned it slowly, bracing himself as though something terrifying lay in wait on the other side.

"Go on, Alex. It isn't Narnia."

Alex cut his gaze to Ben and offered him a wobbling smile. Then he opened the door and stepped into the dark room.

29

TRISTAN

The bedroom door swung open, ending the longest five minutes of Tristan's life.

Alex entered the room and behind him, Ben, who hit the switch, lighting up the room.

Alex looked around at the room which, except for the rose petals strewn everywhere like a windstorm blew them in an open window, was unchanged.

"Surprise!" Tristan said, opening his arms. He wasn't naked, yet but that part would hopefully come next.

"Um…" Alex looked around again. "Okay?" He looked at Ben. "I'm so confused. Are surprises supposed to be this confusing?"

Tristan laughed and approached Alex.

"Once upon a time, there was a boy who loved another boy. And though these boys fell desperately in love, they broke up. One boy moved away, and by the time he came back, the other boy had married. But those boys, you see, they fell in love with the boy who came back."

"There's a lot of boys in this story." Alex's smile was shy and his cheeks tinted pink as Ben's hands settled on his hips. "If I didn't already know the story, I might get confused."

"Shhh. You're interrupting." Tristan cleared his throat and began again. "The boy and his husband wanted to keep the boy who came back. They wanted to keep him for forever. But this boy, he didn't want to live in the king's bedroom."

"Now we're kings?" Ben chuckled behind Alex.

"Shush. Yes, we're kings. Why would you doubt that we're royalty? Anyway," Tristan shot Ben a look that he hoped told him to shut his trap, lovingly. "Anyway, the kings decided they had a spare room in their chambers for the boy who came back. And they asked him once upon a time to share their chambers. But the boy didn't. And the kings understood. But many months had passed, and the kings thought it was high time their third king, because he is a king, moved into their chambers with him."

"Tristan…" Alex breathed his name as Ben pressed a kiss to the curve of Alex's neck.

"We moved your stuff in here this morning. You sleep here anyway. For all intents and purposes, this was already your room, we just made it official."

Tristan grasped Alex's cheeks in his hands and pulled him into a kiss. He kissed him until he felt Alex relent, until his body went limp and lax and melted into the kiss. He'd get his own way; he knew he would.

Alex pulled away and a glassy eyed gaze met Tristan's. "How does the story end?"

Tristan kissed the corner of Alex's mouth. "The third boy became a king and joined his fellow kings in their chambers. It was silly not to, he realized, because they had room for him. Room in the closet and the bed, and in their hearts. Spare room where he fit perfectly, completing them in ways they'd only dreamed of.

"But the best part of the story," Ben said. "Is that it doesn't end. The three kings live together, loving each other, not giving up on each other, and their story doesn't end. Some chapters are more exciting than others. But nothing ends."

"I like that." Alex's voice cracked as he choked back his emotions.

"I do too."

"I don't think I hate surprises anymore," Alex confessed with a watery laugh.

"You don't hate anything we do." Tristan stepped closer and slid his arms around Alex. He dropped his head on Alex's shoulder and breathed deeply, steadying his rocky, but elated, emotions.

"I hate it when you leave the cap off the toothpaste." Alex shot back.

"Okay, so you hate one thing I do. That's not a bad track record."

"So was this the whole surprise, or is there more, because honestly… I'm feeling a little underwhelmed."

Tristan straightened up and looked at Ben. "Can you believe his gratitude? Why it's too much, Ben. I don't know how he can contain his excitement."

Alex opened his mouth to reply, but a rustling noise caught his attention. He turned to the closet. "What the fuck?"

Tristan feigned stupidity. "Maybe something fell. We sort of chucked your stuff in there. I was going to sort it later for you."

Alex rolled his eyes and stepped away from them, toward the closet. "Yeah. Okay. Because that's romantic."

Alex opened the door and a furry ball of wiggle came out, weaving itself around his legs, sniffing and yipping with sudden excitement as Alex stood and gaped down at it. Then he slowly knelt and gathered the little ball of fur and tongue up in his arms.

"Oh my god," he whispered. "Hello, there. Hi, sweety. Oh, my god." He looked up at Ben and Tristan who stood there with twin, shit-eating grins on their faces.

"Surprise," Ben said, sliding an arm around Tristan's waist. They'd talked about a dog a few times over the years, but between the store and Tristan's shifts, they didn't feel confident that they had enough time for one. But with Alex around, for sure, their new addition would get plenty of love and attention.

"What's her name? His name? Oh, my god. Is this real?" Alex looked down at the little dog.

"Her name is Bailey, and she's a two-and-a-half year old shelter dog. Her previous owners surrendered her because they were moving and couldn't take her. No one knows exactly what breed she is."

"That's okay. She's perfect." Alex laughed as Bailed wriggled up closer and licked at his face. "I'm so torn now, though, because I want to strip naked and shower you two with appreciation, but I also want to lie on the floor all day and play with Bailey."

"Well, you can do both. But first, why don't we all take Bailey out for a walk, and maybe when she's tired enough we can come back here and work on that other idea of yours." Ben suggested.

Alex didn't move right away. He sat and stroked his fingers through Bailey's tan fur while she continued to wriggle and lick him.

Alex looked up at them, then got to his feet. Bailey circled the room, sniffing and exploring. "It's funny, but you didn't mention the king's adopting a dog in the story." Alex stepped into Tristan's waiting arms.

"After the boy moved into the kings' bedchambers, they gave him a dog, and though one husband swore the dog would sleep in a crate, he knew he'd cave eventually and let the new member of their family sleep in the bed with them, dog hair be damned."

"And they lived happily ever after." Alex added.

"Yes," Tristan agreed, brushing a kiss against Alex's lips. "They did."

"Good," said Alex. "That's the best part."

The End

ABOUT THE AUTHOR

E. M. Denning is a married mom of three and a writer from British Columbia. Author of endearing filth and schmoopy sex, also addicted to books and coffee. She writes romance for the 18+ crowd.

Follow her on Facebook
Subscribe to her newsletter
Join her Facebook group Denning's Darlings

ALSO BY E.M. DENNING

The Desires Series

What He Needs

What He Craves

What He Hides

What He Fears

Upstate Education Series

Half As Much

More Than Anything

Never Enough

Learning the Ropes

Everything to Lose

Nothing to Gain

The Blackburn Brothers Duet

The Sweetest Thing

The Secret Thing

Standalones

Best Laid Plans

Murder Husbands

Lust and Longing

Collaborations

With Kate Hawthorne

Irreplaceable

Future Fake Husband

Future Gay Boyfriend

Future Ex Enemy

With Kate Hawthorne and E.M. Lindsey

Cloudy with a Chance of Love

Made in the USA
Middletown, DE
29 December 2024